VINDICATED
BY HIS
GRACE

THE FINAL BOOK OF THE FORGIVENESS SERIES

Vindicated by his Grace

THE FINAL BOOK OF THE FORGIVENESS SERIES

SHANI J. MIXON

Acknowledgements

I thank God for my life, for my family, for my friends, for the mountains, for the valleys, and for you... I could continue on and I would run out of pages. God is good and my prayer is that you will see His Glory in this story.

To my husband, Jay, I love you so much. Do you remember when the minister asked me why I wanted to marry you? What did I say? I said, "I love Jay. His love for God makes me want to know God even more." I still mean that. Thank you for always supporting and believing in me. M.E. Productions all the way!

Thank you, Mother, for making me dot all my i's and cross all my t's. Mom, you will always be my English teacher. You've started me on this journey of writing.

To my dearest children, all of you, never give up your dreams, even when the storm is relentless. Water is needed for a seed to sprout. So, go sing in the rain. Then dance in the puddles. You bring me joy. I love you.

Special Thanks

Special thanks to my editor, Michelle. You are amazing! Your professionalism, friendliness, and honest feedback have been a positive catapult in my writing journey.

Thank you to Kim from KILA Designs. When I first saw your design work, I fell in love. Thank you for creating a visual that surpassed my own thoughts. Love it!

And to Liam Ellis, the model on the cover, who is the face of Corey. Thanks for your diligence, hard work, and love for God!

Behold, I have erected the smith who blows the fire of coals and produces a weapon for its purpose. I have also created the ravager to destroy; no weapon that is fashioned against you shall succeed, and you shall refute every tongue that rises against you in judgment. This is the heritage of the servants of the Lord and their vindication from me, declares the Lord.
Isaiah 54:16-17 ESV

And Tennessee became the smith and Andrew the ravager...

Prologue

TENNESSEE coolly sat in his chair and peered at the blue-eyed man in front of him. Impeccable style and swagger exuded from his visitor like a strong cologne lingering enough to entice the senses. An expensive suit hung on his body like a girlfriend—fitting and sexy. There was no rivalry between them, but more of a silent admiration. Although Tennessee had little experience in the market of his guest, both men were willing to die to obtain money and power. Now an offer lay on the table that couldn't be turned down. He'd be a fool to say no. He wasn't planning to say no.

"So, let me get this straight. You want me to take care of a million dollars and you're willing to give me ten percent," Tennessee said.

"Yes, I'm a reasonable man. I don't need anything tied to me, and my connect is no longer around."

"And what makes you think I can do this? Don't get me wrong, I mean, I admire the idea that you believe I can. It's just that, well, we don't really know one another. You know of me. I know of you, but that's about it," Tennessee pushed.

"Hmmm. That's true, but let's just say I have a source that says you can. Well, maybe not you, but someone you know and someone that I'd like to get to know."

"And who might that be?" Tennessee moved his body forward. Eyebrows quirked.

"A woman by the name of Mia. I heard she can move money like the wind. I need that right about now."

"Oh." Tennessee took a deep breath thinking of the beauty. He hated that she didn't take a chance. "She is no longer in my reach. That was a while ago."

"Yes, but a source of mine tells me you know where to find her. I want nothing but the best. And I'm thinking she is the best."

"Fifteen," Tennessee interjected as his hand grabbed his chin.

"Come again?" The man leaned toward Tennessee.

"Fifteen percent. I have to do some leg work. She'll not be easy to get," Tennessee admitted.

"Well, I know that you're a resourceful man and the streets say that whatever Tennessee wants, he gets."

"And these streets don't lie." Tennessee smiled.

"It'll be nice doing business with you, Tennessee."

"And likewise, Andrew." Tennessee smiled as his plan to get Mia began to unfold.

Chapter One

Do not lie to one another, seeing that you have put off the old self with its practices. Colossians 3:9 ESV

THE sweet taste of the cigarillo marinated on Corey's palate as he held the heat in his mouth. Staring ahead at the small lake in the back of his home, he watched white smoke push into the air as he exhaled. Even though his smoking eased his nerves, he could still hear the voice of his dead mother warning him about smoking. Corey wondered at what point had he taken on the habit of his father. The answer came quickly. A month ago. His supervisor called him in the office and easily dismissed him from a career that once crowned him as a promising young professional.

A recent human resource audit determined Corey had lied on his resume. His dishonesty gave him paid administrative leave. He was grateful for the compensation while the firm determined his fate. Unfortunately, their generosity didn't last long. After four weeks, the payments stopped. His last check sat in his account as bills quickly snatched their hefty portions. In thirty days time, his wife and children would be without medical benefits, and that scared him.

Corey wondered whether he should've been truthful. Lying about having a few entry level positions as a financial analyst seemed to encourage the lucrative marketing company to take a chance on an ex thug. Not to mention that they knew he was married to Mia, one of the most renowned accountants in Circle City. Yet, somehow his hard work and his wife's name wasn't enough to have them overlook his lie.

Taking a long drag of his cigar, Corey shook his head. Not even recruiting two high profile clients within the last month and voluntarily training two interns without compensation granted him leniency. The board only saw his indiscretion as lame leg or sore thumb. His repeated apologies had fallen on deaf ears.

Maybe it was fair, he guessed. To admit his fame of being one of the best dope dealers in Cali wouldn't rest well with his newfound circle. Dope boys were business men, too. Successful ones were managers, trainers, investors, financers, and regulators. If that were counted, he would have a decade worth of experience in the business world, but to consider his illegal actions would be absurd. The board would get back to him soon with a final answer. That would have to be enough.

A smirk formed on Corey's mouth as he looked at the three lonely zeros tagging behind a single digit number on his online bank statement. Two years ago, money like this would be considered an insult. He could spend those short figures in a matter of minutes on a few pairs of shoes and a possible outfit. What he gave up to becoming a man of God, a husband, and a father had come at a huge sacrifice. If he was at it, Mia and his children would be living like royalty and there would be no worries about foreclosed houses, repossessed cars, and canceled medical benefits. That wasn't him anymore.

He'd found God after staring at the end of a smoking gun and vowed to never go back to the unforgiving streets. Right now, it appeared as if God was giving him another spiritual reality check and frankly, he wasn't ready for a second round. This round might go to the devil, if he was pressed enough. He'd been poor and desperate. That wasn't an option.

Corey decided against telling Mia about his termination. She was busy basking in a three month leave from a demanding job to spend time with their new son, Corey, Jr. Lying to her about working from home came easy. He remembered it like yesterday.

"Baby, you home, today?" Mia walked in the kitchen looking delectable. Her short, floral robe stopped mid-thigh allowing Corey to get an eyeful of her firm,

long legs. Her hair lay in loose ringlets after being freshly freed from bantu knots.

"Yes, baby. I'm home for a while," Corey said, looking over the rim of his coffee. He's been sitting at the kitchen table scrolling through job listings online.

"Hmm, how long?" Mia leaned over his cup and peeked at his phone.

Grateful that he already knew she would be nosey, he'd closed the job window and pulled up his photo gallery. "I'll be here for a while. I wanted to surprise you. I got paid paternity leave. One of my job perks." The bitterness of his lie quickly filled him with regret.

Mia's hips swayed back and forth in her happy dance before sitting on his lap. "I'm so happy, baby."

The fabricated story had Mia on cloud nine. The house stayed clean. He woke up to breakfast, lunch, dinner, and dessert. Even their intimacy sored. So, on most days he would spend countless hours behind his home computer filling out online job applications.

Corey stepped on the cigar and pitched it into the pond, then went inside the house to retrieve his car keys. Mia was at her parents' house with CJ and Taylor, giving him what she thought was time to finish financial reports in peace and quiet. He needed to get out and figure out how to get money. Mia just took three hundred dollars out of their shared account to shop for the kids. Any other time, her consensual withdrawal would have left a smile on his face, but this time the deduction made his blood pressure rise in anticipation of their mortgage, two car payments, tuition, and other small bills that would surely follow.

His desire was to see Mia happy. She deserved it after all the hell she'd been through. She didn't need another dead weight knocking her off her throne. Corey swore he'd never be that guy. Mia was his other half and there was no way he would be leaning on her to take care of him. It didn't matter that she made more than double his yearly salary. He paid the bills and there was no compromise. His father, Adrian, hadn't taught him much, but what he did do was remind him to be self-sufficient every day of his life for over a decade.

After jumping in his RLS Audi, it didn't take long to get to the home of his adopted little brother, Jamal. He spied him wiping down a fresh set of rims in his driveway.

"I see you, boy." Corey jumped out the driver's seat and looked at the yellow custom rims on Jamal's Charger.

"Hmm. Yep, trying to stay fresh in this small city. I'm still representing Cali all day. Sunshine State forever, baby." Jamal stood.

"Yeah, I didn't realize they were paying you like that at your job, bro." Corey smiled as he bent down to look at his reflection in the wheels.

"Yep, I got a night job. It keeps a little extra in my pocket." Jamal patted his pants.

"I might have to get on where you are," Corey said.

"No, you don't. You already have a job that pays you good. You've been there for over a year and have a huge place," Jamal said as he walked around his car to wipe another rim.

"Yeah, well, I don't know," Corey muttered.

Jamal stood to watch his mentor. "What's up, man? I mean, this isn't you. You always have a plan."

Corey looked at the young man that he had taken under his wing after they escaped the claws of Tennessee. Their lives had been connected far beyond mutual likings. They had a past that would bind them forever.

"I lost my job." Corey cut straight to the chase.

"How?" Jamal stopped wiping his rims.

"I lied, man. I told them that I worked for a few companies in California. I couldn't tell them that I had no experience in corporate America. I mean, I was a financial analyst for my father's empire and we made millions, but that wouldn't look good on my resume."

"How do you know?" Jamal smiled.

"You're playing. I'm for real," Corey responded, but a hint of mirth danced in his eyes.

"Sorry, man. Look. You're smart. You can get another job. Plus, Mia's a good woman. She'll understand," Jamal said.

"I haven't been exactly truthful with her. She thinks I'm still working. We have a family. I can't put that stress on her and the kids."

"No offense, but she can take care of you all without your paper. Man, she can take care of all of us, truth be told," Jamal said, pointing to himself and his mother's house.

"That's my wife, my family. I'm supposed to take care of them."

"Yeah, well, taking care of your family doesn't just mean financially. You need to take care of Mia physically, emotionally, all that mess they talk about in those women magazines. She already had a dude to lie, steal, and cheat on her. She doesn't need another brother lying to her as well," Jamal said.

"I'm going to tell her tonight and let the chips fall where they may, but I'm serious about that job, bruh," Corey said.

"Nah, man, this work ain't for you. It's too stressful. I'm telling you. I can hook you up with my daytime connect. It's nothing close to what you've been getting, but its honest and it'll help pay the bills until that company of yours realizes they made a huge mistake in letting you go."

"Yeah. I know. So, how is Nikki doing?"

"She's hanging in there. She likes this lame city. She's even trying to date a bit, but I'm not feeling that at all. These dudes out here see my momma and go crazy. Man, I hate that. These old cats out here are disrespectful." Jamal shook his head.

Corey laughed. "I mean, would you rather her be ugly? Your mom is a smart woman. She knows who's going to treat her right and who is out here to get it in."

"Yeah, but these dudes at the church though! The day she walked in the place, all single guys over thirty started acting like they could be holy escorts around town. Then when they found out she could sing, oh, it was over."

Corey's stomach bubbled in laughter. "I know. I do remember that. Pastor had to have a talk with a few of the guys. First Lady Michelle had to put a few of these insecure wives in check, too, thinking Nikki was out to get their husbands."

"Crazy!" Jamal shook his head.

"So, what's up with you and church? You were hanging in there for a while. Now, you do pop ups and visit B.S.C. when they have special services."

"B.S.C.? What is that?" Jamal asked.

"Man, Bedside Church," Corey said.

"You stupid!" Jamal laughed.

"Okay, but still you there, right?" Corey smiled.

"Look, I love God, but I'm not trying to be up in there. I'm not feeling it. I mean, it's too much protocol. You gotta call people titles and pay all your money to a man who is rich from your suffering.

Man, I'm good. Pastor got my money up in there buying cars and houses and I can't even get one. Man, please." Jamal huffed.

Corey shook his head as he thought of how much he used to be like Jamal. He looked at the young brother and wanted to tell him all the things he could be doing, but talk was cheap. He learned that a long time ago. Talking went in one ear and out the other, especially when someone had his mind made up already. Experience would soon be Jamal's teacher.

"Alright, I have to go before my wife gets home. I told her that I'd be at the office for only a minute. So…"

"Yeah, you have to keep this lie going. You ain't right, man. Handle your business. Tell her the truth," Jamal said.

"I know. I will. I'll tell her the truth and then you come to church with me on Sunday." Corey attempted to negotiate.

"I can't make any promises, but what I can do is say that I'll think about it," Jamal stated.

"Cool." Corey realized that was a start.

Chapter Two

Yet you do not know what tomorrow will bring. What is your life? For you are a mist that appears for a little time and then vanishes. JAMES 4:14 ESV

MIA stared at little sleeping CJ. His small, chocolate body was perfectly formed. Touching the soft skin of his chunky leg that stuck out from his onesie made her smile. Midnight black curls covered his head and Mia calmed her urge to touch them. CJ would wake up and he needed his nap.

The moment the doctors put him on her chest three months ago, she fell in love with Corey's miniature replica. She was a proud mother and grateful that God had given her another chance at marriage. Life had thrown her lemons a while ago and now she was drinking lemon-ade on ice through a bendable straw. She hadn't forgotten about her past pain, but Mia recognized it as a rocky path that brought to her life with Corey, Taylor, and CJ.

After CJ was born, she often wondered why she and Edward never had a child. He most definitely wanted one. Truthfully, she was glad that a child had never come from their union. She adopted Edward's daughter, Taylor. That had been enough. Taylor never met her biological mother and it was for the best. The tragedy of being a product of divorce and a flaky social media model mother would be too much to bear for a child. Tay'Von "Lollibae" Harris, social media mogul, gave Edward a great run in college. Their fling produced a child which she left for Edward to raise. When Edward met Mia, he'd come with a child that she would end up calling her very own.

Smiling, Mia left CJ in his crib and walked to her bedroom. She loved her new home in the northern suburb of Carmel. She and Corey purchased the colonial style home almost a year ago after selling the house that she and her ex once shared.

Mia pulled out a small familiar box from her nightstand and headed to the bathroom. She sat down on the edge of the tub. Her heart began to thump faster as she used her nail to pop the box top open. She pulled out the plastic wrapped test strip and read the directions. She'd seen the words before, but it was her nervousness that caused her to review the instructions as if it were the first time. Her period had only been a few days late. She was in denial that only after two months of ending breastfeeding, she could possibly get pregnant. CJ was only three months old and she was scheduled to go back to work in two weeks. Having another baby was not in the plan, but she would love to have another. Truthfully, she wouldn't mind retiring her career to be a stay at home mom to an entire tribe of little Coreys. She loved her life and desperately desired just to be a wife who took care of home. Butterflies whizzed in her stomach, knowing that CJ would not be close even if he would be spending the day with his grandmother. She even enjoyed being home when Taylor came home from school. Her stepdaughter was close to becoming a teenager and growing up so quickly.

"Two lines mean pregnant. One line means not pregnant," Mia read aloud and peeled the plastic from the strip.

Mia prayed that Corey wouldn't be too shocked if the results came back positive. The last time they talked, Corey said he wanted five kids. But that revelation came after watching a movie about a house full of loving kids. She agreed that they should have a house full, but never did she imagine that they would be popping them out back to back. They planned CJ, not this potential one.

She listened to the steady stream of urine as it hit the strip.

"Babe, where you at?" Mia was pulled from her thoughts as Corey called her name.

"Upstairs," she hollered back as she quickly set the test on the sink and rinsed her hands.

Hurried footsteps made their way upstairs. "Babe." Corey entered the bedroom.

"Hi, baby." Mia smiled, admiring his dark chocolate features. Silky, unblemished skin reminded her of precious onyx stone. His locks were long gone. Now a line up haircut stood in its place along with a thick, impeccable beard.

"Why are you standing their looking at me like that?" Corey asked.

"I was just thinking how fine my man is. You have me over here blushing."

"Woman, don't start nothing in here. Taylor will be home soon, and CJ will wake up," Corey said while gently pulling Mia's hand to bring her closer. He kissed her lips and then stood back to look at her.

"Dinner will be done soon. I have a steak going for you." Mia touched both of his arms and batted her eyes.

"Mia, I'm serious. Stop looking at me like that." Corey laughed.

"Oh, so you act like you don't want me." Mia pouted.

"Wife, I want you every day, but like I said, Taylor will be walking in here any minute and CJ will be blocking. So, let's take a rain check for later." Corey walked toward the bathroom.

Mia's heart stopped. She hadn't planned to have Corey see the pregnancy test. She wanted to know the results first. If it read negative, there would be no need for a discussion. If the test was positive, then she had planned to tell him later in the evening after she could process the situation. Now, there'd be a conversation regardless the outcome and she wasn't ready for that.

A million questions raced through her mind and there were no answers. The chime of the door interrupted her thoughts. Taylor was home and her usual first stop was to check on her mother.

"Mom!" Taylor hollered. "Are you upstairs?"

"Yes."

"Is Pop here, too?" Taylor asked about Corey.

"Yes," Mia responded.

CJ started crying and Mia sighed. Their voices woke him up a bit early from his nap.

"I'll get him," Taylor called.

Mia was grateful.

The bathroom door slowly opened, and Corey held the test strip in his hand. Steely eyes studied the strip and his stoic expression made his face unreadable. Mia prepared for his disappointment.

"Corey?" Mia said

His hooded gaze and slight rise and fall of his chest made Mia wonder if he was attempting to calm himself down or go into an unexpected rage. The latter was impossible; Corey was not a man of fury.

"Corey?" Mia called again.

"Congratulations, we're going to be parents again." Corey smiled, yet the happiness didn't seem to reach his eyes.

"What? Mom, you're pregnant? This is too much. You just had a baby." Taylor walked in the room holding CJ.

Mia mentally punched herself for not closing the bedroom door. The entire household stood in silence, including little CJ.

"I'm getting your steak out the oven." Mia's voice was barely audible in the tension filled room.

"Mom, am I having steak, too?" Taylor asked, impervious to the drama.

Mia sighed. This day hadn't gone as planned. This was unexpected.

"Tomorrow will start a new day. Hopefully, it will get better," Mia whispered to herself.

Chapter Three

He is a double-minded man, unstable in all his ways.
JAMES 1:8 ESV

*A*ND *Tyler became double-minded.*
Tyler Deen was tired of talking to the clueless detectives about the death of his sister, Peyton. After months, there was no lead into how she ended up stripped of her clothes with two bullet wounds in her back on a secluded beach somewhere in Hollywood. Tyler knew Peyton's estranged boyfriend, Andrew, had something to do with it. However, there was no proof and his lawyers warned him against searching for evidence that would sentence an already twisted and demented man such as Andrew. The Deen family had money for good legal representation, but Andrew's money was long as twenty football fields and his goons were much more powerful. They were lethal.

Peyton had been wooed by Andrew through an online dating site over a year ago. He pounced on her at her weakest moment and she fell victim to his deceptive ways. He filled her void of depression unto death.

The Deen family was still in shock, and his parents, Charles and Amelia, were hit the hardest. Amelia Deen, once the outspoken heiress of Green Pastures, was under the watchful eye of a psychiatrist and relied on Melody, her daughter-in-law, nearly each day to get through simple routines as taking a shower with soap. Charles Deen had taken an immediate and indefinite leave of absence and left a mega church in the hands of his son, Tyler.

The Pennsylvania campus was now put on hold and the weight of the world sat on Tyler's tired shoulders. His new wife, Melody, was his breath of fresh air and their dreams to quickly add children to their family were vanishing. Melody said she could handle carrying a baby, but the stress of caring for his mother might cause a miscarriage and he couldn't tolerate another loss. They had little Lena, his wife's daughter with her ex, to look after and she was usually under the constant care of her nanny.

Never in a million years did Tyler believe he would be senior pastor of Green Pasture's main campus with a congregation close to four thousand people before the age of thirty. After he and Melody married, people came in droves to be a part of a church that was the face of interracial faith. Tyler was a white pastor of a mega church who fell in love with a black woman. He hadn't noticed her color when he first met Melody, but what he did see was a gorgeous woman with a heart of gold.

The news of Peyton's tragic death spread like a raging wildfire through the church community and hundreds of people left Green Pastures in suspicion that there was more to the story than what the Deen family was willing to release. Most believed Peyton had been a victim of a violent robbery gone wrong. Speculators and naysayers were convinced drug and alcohol abuse were involved. The Deen's remained tight-lipped and would not reveal the last days of Peyton's life.

The truth was that Peyton's death had left their family in ruins, and Tyler had become the glue in the family as his father shattered into a million pieces while helping the struggling Amelia to want to wake up each day.

"I love you." Tyler felt the soft weight of his wife's arms around his neck.

Turning from his computer, he gave a long and slow once over of the brown beauty smiling at him. She was his queen and he was forever grateful that God had given him such a woman. She married into this family not knowing that such a misfortune would hit them so soon. Late into the night, he could hear the prayers of his wife thanking God for her new family and God's extended grace and mercy over them. With her prayers, a bit of guilt resonated within him knowing that she'd become much more than a wife, but the light that gave a dying Deen family hope.

"I love you, too, Mrs. Deen." Tyler's eyes lit up and he pulled Melody to his lap. He inhaled deeply to capture her familiar scent of soft lavender.

"I brought your dinner to you. I don't want it to get cold," Melody said as she touched his face and placed a plate of food on his desk.

Tyler frowned. "What time is it?" He hoped he hadn't let time slip away again.

"No worries, baby." Melody smiled.

Looking at the clock on the wall, Tyler noticed the time was well past eight. He was an hour and a half late for dinner.

"I'm sorry, sweetheart. I didn't know it was this late. Why didn't you come get me?" he asked.

"Don't worry yourself. I've been busy, too. I packed dinner for Mom and Dad and took it to them." Melody smiled again.

Tyler was grateful that his wife and parents had put their differences behind them. Before he and Melody were married, both Charles and Amelia were not willing to accept a black woman as their daughter-in-law. Their ignorance nearly cost Tyler his relationship, but now Melody had become a second daughter to Charles and Amelia. He was thankful that living in the guest house to his parents' home was not a problem for Melody. The four-bedroom home was enough to remain separate from his parents but close enough to tend to their growing needs.

"I thought Darrya would be cooking dinner." Tyler asked about the family cook and house attendant.

"I gave her a day off. She has been practically working around the clock since… you know." Melody hesitated to mention his sister.

"I know. I guess I should've thought of that," Tyler said.

"You've enough to think about," Melody said

"Yes, I mean I think about you all day and how much I want to hold you and touch you."

"Oh really?" Melody glowed.

"Yes, and how much I want to thank you for sticking by my side." Tyler looked to Melody.

"Anything for you, for us," Melody responded.

"You're my rib," Tyler said. He could feel his eyes burn but refused to let one tear drop. He hadn't cried in the months since Peyton died, and he wasn't planning to be an emotional catastrophe in front of his wife. He was now the head of this family and he had to be strong.

"You're a good man. You've taken on much responsibility. God selected you because of your strength and your faithfulness to Him, but the righteous can cry out. The bible says, 'When the righteous cry for help, the Lord hears and delivers them out of all their troubles.' Tyler, you can cry out." Melody touched his chest.

Wrapping his arms around her, Tyler allowed the silent tears to flow. He didn't plan on this evening ending up like this, but the pressure was building. Holding her had been his undoing just as he fell hopelessly in love the moment she walked into Green Pastures nearly a year ago. He always wondered how such a woman could influence him. He was jelly around her.

"I want you to come up in a while. You've been sitting here most of the day researching leads to Peyton's death. We already know who did this." Melody's voice was calm. Yet, it held finality.

"I know, but I need a way to get to him. You know this, babe. Mom and Dad are blaming themselves." Tyler released his wife just a bit.

"This is no one's fault but the person who pulled the trigger. Let me ask you this. What would you do if you could prove that Andrew did this? Then what?" Melody asked.

A brief silence permeated the room along with the ticking clock and Tyler's heavy breathing. How could he tell his wife that he desperately wished to harm Andrew for changing their lives so much? If one more person said they were praying for his family, he was going to lose it. Grateful he was for the prayers, he was tired of the pitiful stares and unapologetic questions.

"Tyler?"

"I don't know." Tyler blinked.

"Vengeance is mine said the Lord," Melody quoted.

"You're preaching to the choir. I know what has been said. I'm just doing a little research. The bible also says that the soul of the sluggard craves and gets nothing, while the soul of the diligent is richly supplied. I'm diligently trying to find evidence against the... against a killer." Tyler struggled to not curse.

Melody sighed. "Didn't you just preach a sermon about how people misinterpret the bible for their own personal gain and how they'll have to answer to the Lord?"

Melody started to stand, but Tyler gently held her in place. "Baby, I'm sorry. You're right. I'll be done in a few. Take my dinner back to the dining room. I'm going to eat it there."

Melody kissed him and stood to walk out the room. "I love you."

"I love you more."

Melody exited the room and he watched the door close. A bit of guilt traveled through him knowing that she worried. He didn't want her thinking about what he would do once solid proof pointed Andrew's way. Tyler believed himself to be a man of God, but flesh was ruling heavily in bringing that murderer to his knees. Rest would not come until Andrew's empire was eradicated.

The buzz of his phone pulled Tyler from his relentless thoughts. The notification was for an unread text message. Unlocking his phone, Tyler's adrenaline rushed when he read it.

> *Meet me at my office ASAP.*
> *I've got pics.*

Tyler jumped to his feet. His private investigator was worth every expensive penny. He only prayed what the guy had was enough. He exited the office entrance to his home and quickly forgot about his wife and dinner waiting.

Chapter Four

A man of quick temper acts foolishly and a man of evil devices is hated. PROVERBS 14:17 ESV

MELODY'S temper rose. Tyler left her in the dining room without as much as goodbye while he played cops and robbers. It was close to 12:00 a.m. when he entered the house like a thief in the night. She was even more angry about the idea of him believing that she thought he never left. This obsession with Andrew was killing everyone which defeated the purpose of trying to get some chance at justice. Melody wanted to see Andrew in jail, but in the meantime, the Deen family needed to begin a course of healing.

Even amid irritation, Melody mastered the art of smiling, nodding, and appearing to be calm. Fake it until you make it is the motto she learned quickly. Being a first lady was hard work, especially when her every move was scrutinized. It was Thursday night and Green Pastures was packed for midweek service. She sat in the pulpit and listened to Tyler preach a soul shaking Word about faith. He was saying some powerful stuff about this walk with the Lord, but Melody wondered if he even believed what came out of his mouth. The congregation sure did because they were on their feet five minutes into the message.

As Tyler finished his sermon, Melody stood, waving her hand in reverence. The classic hands in the air praise was deserved, but she was really just ready to get some air. She missed the privacy of her condominium near downtown Chicago. She and Tyler owned two properties that they would be subletting. Perhaps she could go there for a while after church and eat dinner there with Lena.

The plan was to sell their homes in a year and use the money to build their dream home in Pennsylvania. At the rate they were going, they would be living in the Deen's guest house for years.

"Amen," Melody mechanically said along with the entire congregation as Tyler ended with prayer.

Melody quickly walked to the back exit before her husband. She wanted to get to her car without any conversation. Walking swiftly with her two-man security team on her heals, she could make an exit without much talking at all.

"Melody!" Tyler shouted as she exited the building. The breeze caught her skirts, and she didn't seem to care as her thighs were exposed to the world. Yes, she was mad.

Sucking her teeth, Melody responded, "Yes?"

"What are you doing? Where are you going?" He approached her and shielded his eyes from the glaring sun.

"I need some air, Tyler."

"Why? We have plans to eat with my parents."

"And we had plans to eat dinner last night in our dining room, but that didn't happen. And now you want me to sit in the cold home of your parents and eat a sad meal?"

"Come on, Melody, I...I didn't mean for that to happen like that last night. Baby, I need answers and you know my parents need us right now."

"And I need my husband!" Melody's voice was loud, and it caused more than a few heads to turn. Melody gestured for the security to give them space. She trusted them to keep their family business private, but she still needed them to go.

"Give us a minute," Tyler requested. The men nodded and headed toward the backdoor entrance to stand.

"Okay. Okay. I don't want you to go. Lets you and I spend some time together. I'll tell my parents that we'll see them later." Tyler was close to begging.

"I don't know."

"Melody, that wasn't me asking you. Give me a minute and I'll be ready." Tyler gestured for one of the security team to make sure Melody got in the car safely.

Her eyebrow quirked in his assertiveness, but she respected his authority in making a solid decision. If he would've let her go, she'd probably become angrier. The truth was that she needed time with her husband, not sitting by her lonesome eating a bland frozen dinner.

Once inside her car, Melody rested her head on the soft cushion of the headrest. As she tried to relax, her muscles tensed again when she noticed Tyler's ex fake fiancé leaving through the administrative side of the church. Looking at the tight fitted bodycon dress that hugged every curve, Melody immediately concluded that the woman must have gotten breast augmentation. Kelly's once B cups were now spilling out a triple D cup. Her perky set were on display for the world to see and right now her world was Tyler. Kelly had been livid when Tyler broke off their engagement. Her bitterness had turned into a passive aggressiveness toward Melody.

"Why is she here? And why is she leaving out the office exit?" Melody sighed.

Melody expelled a breath of frustration and hit her fist on the dashboard. Today was not the day for being a jealous woman, but little Miss Curvy was sashaying a bit too hard toward Tyler. She tried to close her eyes and count to ten. Melody slowly opened her eyes and Kelly was talking to Tyler which caused Melody to jump out the car. The strong taps of her heels interrupted Kelly's calculated conversation. A smile curved her lips although she wanted to frown and smack Kelly.

"Hi, love." Melody locked arms with Tyler and gave Kelly a penetrating stare.

Tyler was oblivious to Melody's internal irritation. He pulled her a bit closer and kissed her cheek. The subtle move immediately saturated the rage of fire brewing within her.

"Oh, Melody. It's so nice to see you," Kelly crooned as her eyes traveled from Melody's hair to the tips of her toes.

"Kelly, wow, it's been a long time since I've seen you." Melody tried not to rest her eyes on Kelly's chest.

"Oh." Kelly giggled. "It has. Hasn't it? I was just telling Tyler the same thing."

It was on the tip of Melody's tongue to ask if it was necessary to mention her lack of presence to Tyler by the administrative entrance. Kelly lingering by the door appeared a bit calculated.

"Yes. Well, Tyler, we should get going." Melody tugged at Tyler's arm.

Tyler winked back. "Okay, sweetheart."

"Goodbye, Kelly, and take care," Melody said.

"I might be back next Sunday." Kelly smiled briefly at Melody and gave Tyler a lingering look.

Melody wanted to direct her to another church two suburbs away but dismissed the idea. She was in no place to tell someone to not come to the house of the Lord. Perhaps the woman was on the verge of a breakthrough. However, something told her that is wasn't quite deliverance Kelly was looking to get. Making a mental note to keep a spiritual eye on Kelly, both Melody and Tyler waved as they walked toward the car.

"Thank you, babe." Tyler smiled

"For?" Melody arched an eyebrow.

"Oh, for many things, but for right now, how about supporting me in service today even though you were upset with me, not fighting me about going to dinner together, and not strangling Kelly for starters." Tyler opened the car door for Melody.

"Yes, well, my last name is Deen now. So, I have to represent. I can't act crazy." Melody smiled.

"Right." Tyler closed her door and walked around to the other side.

"So, do you know that I had to cancel two meetings for our quick getaway? Not to mention running from at least fifty people trying to talk to me," Tyler said.

Melody responded by pursing her lips.

Tyler gave directions to their driver to take them to the exclusive Rounders Steakhouse in downtown Chicago. He called and requested a VIP dining suite overlooking the lake. Melody was grateful. She couldn't remember the last time they had been on a dinner date without the company of someone else.

"Thank you for this." Melody beamed.

"I'm sorry for leaving you last night," Tyler said.

"I'm sorry for running out of service," Melody responded.

"Really?" Tyler asked.

"Um, yes." Melody lips curved.

"Give me a kiss then." Tyler smiled and closed the partition.

Melody leaned in to kiss her husband. He wasted no time capturing her in his arms.

Tennessee's flight arrived at Indianapolis International Airport ninety minutes late. With a clenched jaw and quick movement to baggage claim, no one would mistake him for happy. His temper quickened. His plans to pay Mia a visit at Living Waters' 11:00 a.m. service were now null and void. High winds and scattered thunderstorms delayed several flights. Even the impeccable service in first class hadn't curbed his mood.

Just before leaving home, Tennessee spent the entire ride imagining the frightened look on both Mia's and Corey's faces when he walked in the church and enjoyed a bit of Word. It wasn't as if he needed to hear any of the foolishness, but it sure would have been entertaining. It never ceased to amaze Tennessee how people were willing to turn all their faith over to a man who claimed to have a great connection to some higher power. The primitive and vulnerable mindsets of churchgoers left a trail of questions in his mind. Why were these people willing to turn over money to a person that didn't exist? Why do they listen to a book that is full of fairytales as if it were a treasure map to life? Why would these people want to die and go to a place where streets were paved of gold when they could have diamonds and riches in the land of the living? Riches were in the hands of the rich not the ones steady giving up paychecks to prove their loyalty and conjure some bigger blessing.

Tennessee thought of opening his own church and spew lies just to have people pay him to stand in front of them a few times a week. At least it would be legal.

"Tennessee, your room has been checked. It's all clean," a tall man with a solemn appearance spoke through the limousine's intercom.

"Are my towels in the room? Did you change the sheets?" Tennessee asked.

"Yes, they have been pressed and were put on your bed when your flight landed."

"Good," Tennessee said while thinking of his appreciation and need for cleanliness.

"We'll be in the room next door," the man said as he exited to open the passenger door.

"Good, but Martin, keep your distance. No one knows I'm here. I don't want to draw attention with an unnecessary entourage," Tennessee stated.

"You got it." Martin opened the door and proceeded to get his employer's luggage.

Tennessee smirked at Martin's bellhop behavior. The same man had killed for him, now he was running around like house help.

"Is my appointment across the street yet?" Tennessee asked.

"Yes, he arrived early," Martin said.

"I'm going to walk over."

"I wouldn't suggest that. Let me get your bags to the room and I'll walk with you," Martin said.

"I'll be fine. This city doesn't know me. It feels good to just walk without a security team. Check with me in thirty minutes." Tennessee stepped from the car.

He admired the quietness of his surroundings. There was definitely the buzz of urban development, but there was no smog and the busyness of a metropolis.

Tennessee reached the small, secluded bar in no time. He was oblivious to the frequent eyes of women who admired his dark and mysterious appearance. The tailored suit was cut perfectly to emphasize his tall and lean physique.

Tennessee saw his connect and watched as he talked on the phone. The young man stood out like a sore thumb with biker jeans and tubular running shoes. He hadn't seen the kid in close to two years, but yet his thirst to get money had not disappeared. Tennessee inhaled the liquored scent of his surroundings as he prepared for the adrenaline rush to the surprise of a lifetime. It was easy to track a young man who was looking for a quick come up. After throwing the kids name around a few times in Indy, Tennessee had gotten the name of his new employer. Faking a meeting to possible set up shop in Indy, the kid's employer sent him as a scout before a deal could be made.

When their eyes connected, Tennessee nodded and took a seat. It was such a treat to catch a deer in headlights. Now he could just bask in the dilatation of the young man's pupils.

"Jamal, you look so happy to see me." Tennessee smiled.

"What the... How did you find me?" Jamal's voice cracked.

"Come on, man. That question in an insult to both of our intelligences." Tennessee signaled the waitress to their table.

"You're right. What do you want?" Jamal countered.

"That's more like it." Tennessee winked.

"Can I help you?" A petite, brown woman approached the table.

"Give me a neat rye whiskey," Tennessee stated, peering at the woman's golden extensions.

"You got it, honey." She flashed a smile.

"Bring it to me in a paper cup," Tennessee stated.

The waitress nodded and walked away.

"Back to the burning question of why I'm here." Tennessee placed a dab of hand sanitizer in his hands.

"Yeah, back to that," Jamal said.

"Hmmm. You and Corey left so abruptly from what would have had you as second to one of the most powerful cartels in the street. Corey was so ready to denounce the hand that fed him. I was quite convinced you were, too, but, yeah, we both know money is everything." Tennessee watched Jamal. "And by the looks of it, you couldn't resist those greenbacks calling your name. I see the ice on your wrist and fresh new kicks."

"I'm thinking that I'll soon regret my decision."

"Well, once the door is open another one opens, if you know what I mean," Tennessee said.

Jamal shrugged and watched the waitress return to place a paper cup of whiskey on the table. She walked away with her eyes heavenward. Jamal wondered if she thought Tennessee to be strange for requesting a paper cup.

"Oh, so you're now playing the ignorant role. Okay, well, let's get straight to the point. I need Mia back in Cali with me for a while. I have a friend in need of her special services."

"Tennessee, man, that's impossible." Jamal shook his head.

"All things are possible, Jamal. Enlighten me about your confusion."

"Mia is a married woman with two children. She's not jeopardizing her family for a suicide mission. Why would she go back? She has no desire for that type of life anymore," Jamal said.

"Wow, married with children. Beautiful. That would be more of a reason to get a bit of money. Now, I presume, she is married to our friend Corey, correct? "Tennessee beamed.

Jamal didn't respond.

"I'll take that as a yes. I mean, how could Corey leave a beauty like that? So, get this message to your friends. I want Mia on a plane with me in two days. Now, if they say no to this profitable trip, respond this way. Either get on the plane or their love story will end. I'd hate for the kids to be parentless." Tennessee looked at Jamal as his eyes slowly examined the fine sheen of nervous perspiration pushing through the young man's brow.

"End?" Jamal countered.

"I don't have to spell it out for you. End. Dead. Despair. Terminado!" Tennessee stood and put his business card on the table along with a twenty-dollar bill.

Picking up his cup, Tennessee started to take one more last drink, but stopped. A dark crumb sat on the edge of his cup and threw him into a rage. He pitched the cup violently to the ground and walked toward the exit.

"Hey! Man, you can't do that!" The waitress stormed toward Tennessee.

Tennessee stopped mid stride. Anger distorted his dark features into a crazed lunatic. Nostrils flared and teeth bared. His piercing scrutiny anchored the waitress. Before Tennessee could respond, Jamal jumped to his feet and stood in front of the scared woman.

"See there." Tennessee winked at Jamal. "You recognize me for who I am and what I'm capable of."

"Yeah, man. Got you," Jamal said.

"Now, tell this young man thank you. You could have gotten yourself in a lot trouble." Tennessee sneered at the woman.

"Thank you." The woman's voice quivered as she spoke to Jamal.

"Now, if someone asks for a paper cup make sure it's clean!" Tennessee sneered and walked from the bar.

Chapter Five

"For the wages of sin is death..." ROMANS 6:23 ESV

THE swift blades of the ceiling fan Corey lay under cut through the air. He lay on his back to watch them. His thoughts fastened on Mia. Peeking at her through his peripheral vision, he saw the slight rise and fall of her chest. She wasn't sleep, but she wasn't talking either. There was little to say. It gutted Corey to know that he was the cause of his wife's grief for the moment, but he was willing to take this silence then admit to her that he was unemployed.

In the streets, money came easy, but with a price. Damned if you do and damned if you don't. He and Mia had worked so hard on his resume. Then the job offers came as soon as he finished his Associates Degree in Business. Corey was elated. After accepting a lucrative job offer that gave him generous benefits, he told Mia that he wanted to transfer her to his medical plan and take over the payments to the house and car. She didn't bend easily to the idea, but after 10 days of practically begging, she final agreed. Corey just wanted to take the pain and damage away that her ex-husband, Edward, had caused. He wanted his family to want for nothing, and he took pride in being a legitimate provider. Now his wife was pregnant with no benefits. He didn't want her to have to work and be tired from the stress of the job along with carrying a baby.

"Baby?" Mia whispered.

"Yeah, babe, what's up?" Corey said.

"You haven't touched me in like three days and you're distant," Mia said.

Corey took in a deep breath. It was true. He noticed her as she entered the room wearing a peek-a-boo candy red lace negligee. He knew she wanted him thirty minutes ago, but if he opened the doors to his vulnerability, he wouldn't be able to hold on to his secret. They hadn't been intimate for three days and that was unusual for them, but stress was sitting on his shoulders and tapping on his mind.

"I'm sorry, baby." Corey pulled his wife to his chest.

The soft scent of jasmine invaded his nostrils causing a warm feeling to easily fall upon him.

"It would be silly of me to ask you if you're cheating on me. So, I won't, but I do want to know if everything is okay," Mia said.

"You are my infinity. God gave me you, and to you He gave me. I would never do anything to jeopardize what we have. I love you," Corey stated.

"Thank you, baby, but that still doesn't answer my question." Mia slid her hand across Corey's chest and tilted her head to get a better look at him.

Corey held in a laugh. He was in no mood for a smile but thinking of Mia's persistence was a bit funny.

"I have a lot of things on my mind and I'm just in my thoughts. That's all," Corey said.

"I feel like you're disappointed about the baby." Mia's eyes slightly watered.

"I'm not disappointed. I'm just a bit shocked. Don't get me wrong, babe, I want a house full with you, but I just want to make sure we have our finances right," Corey said.

"Our finances are cool. I mean, you are making a pretty good salary and your job gives us great benefits," Mia said.

Corey didn't know how to respond. She was partially right. When he did have a job, there was no sweat about the bills. Now, all he thought about was the lack of money. Maybe it was time to just tell the truth. Living this double life was getting them nowhere.

"Mia?" Corey whispered.

"Shhhh," she softly commanded as she leaned in to kiss Corey.

Her gentle caresses reminded him of what he'd missed for a few days, and he could no longer allow stress to be a barrier to their intimacy. Her touch temporarily eased his doubt. The last wall that he'd placed between them easily came tumbling down. He returned her touch and enjoyed her soft kisses. Just as he was about to pull her closer, a loud bang at the front door jolted them both from the bed.

"What!" Corey looked at the red blaring numbers on the digital clock. It read 1:00 a.m.

"Who do you think it is?" Mia asked as she stood.

"Wait here." Corey stood as well and then put on his robe.

Walking down the hallway, he peeped into CJ's room. Taylor was curled up on a pallet on the floor. She could often be found in her brother's room watching over him. Looking at his son, he felt at peace that he was sound asleep as well. Another bang at the door once again disturbed the peace. Whoever was there better have a good explanation for interrupting what could have been a night to remember.

Corey all but stomped down the stairs as he wondered who on the other side of the door had lost their mind. He looked through the peephole and was surprised to see Jamal.

"Man!" Corey yanked open the door.

"I need to come in, man." Jamal didn't wait for a response as he pushed through the door.

"Jamal!" Corey closed the door and headed toward the couch where Jamal was already seated.

"It's a wrap, dude." Jamal rubbed his hands over his face.

"Man, what's up? I'm confused. Mia 'bout ten second away from coming down here. When she sees you sitting here, she's going to flip, especially if you here for some nonsense. So, if it's something crazy, get it out now." Corey watched the stairs.

"Tennessee is here." Jamal blew out a sigh of frustration.

"What did you say?" Corey's heart exploded into rapid pounding. Dizziness flushed him.

"Tennessee is in town and he wants Mia." Jamal's voice cracked.

"What!" Corey jumped from the couch.

"What is it, baby?" Mia ran down the stairs. Her eyes traveled between Jamal and Corey. Fear and uncertainty held her captive as she waited a response.

"Baby, I told you to wait upstairs." Corey attempted to be calm.

"No, just tell me what's wrong. I can feel something is not right." Mia wrapped her arms around herself.

"You really don't need to be down here," Jamal said.

"It's too late. Did somebody die? What is it? Is it my mom? My dad? Melody? Tell me," Mia nearly screamed.

"It's Tennessee." Corey sighed.

"Okay? What about him? You said that situation was handled a long time ago." Alarm spread across Mia's face.

"I'm not sure. Jamal was in the middle of giving the story." Corey walked toward Mia and placed his arms around her.

"Look. All I know is that Tennessee wants Mia on the plane with him the day after tomorrow. He dropped me his card and that's it." Jamal pulled the business card from his back pocket and placed it on the coffee table.

"And if I refuse?" Mia countered, leaning her head against her husband's chest.

"Refusing is not an option, Mia," Jamal responded with pity.

"Well, she's not going. This is crazy. I mean it's been almost three years, and this guy comes out of nowhere making demands." Corey was quickly losing his cool.

"You already know, man." Jamal shook his head in disdain.

"You know what? I'm thinking like how you even got in contact with Tennessee. I mean, of all people. How did he just randomly choose you?" Corey speculated.

"What are you trying to say?" Jamal instantly became defensive.

"I think you know. I mean, you act like you were at home and Tennessee up and called you out of nowhere. And even if he did, why would you agree to meet him without me?" Corey walked toward Jamal. "So, give me the truth, man. I've known you for too long."

"Corey, bro, I..." Jamal looked from Mia to Corey. Uneasiness had already claimed residence on his face.

"Man, don't make me kill you." Corey grabbed Jamal by his shirt.

"I... man, I don't know what you're talking about," Jamal stammered.

Corey pushed Jamal back into the couch causing the furniture to skate across the floor.

"Corey, stop. This is crazy." Mia's voice caused Corey to turn his attention. "Jamal, please tell us this is just Corey's speculation. I'm pregnant. We have a family. We don't have time for this."

"I can't have my family in jeopardy." Corey let go of Jamal.

"I messed up. I got back in the game a few months ago. I missed the life, man. At twenty-three, I'm working a nine to five to give a chunk to the government, a part to the bills, and the rest to keeping a roof over my head." Jamal could barely look at Corey or Mia.

"So, you got back in the game knowing that road would lead you back to this craziness. Well, not your doom, mine." Corey could barely hold his temper.

"My guy told me a connect wanted to do business with someone new and sent me to scout him out. You know, to see if the guy was legit. It turned out the connect is Tennessee. All he wanted was you." Jamal pointed to Mia.

"Who are you working for?" Corey asked.

"You don't know him," Jamal responded.

"That's not what I asked you," Corey thundered.

"A guy named JT. He's over on the northwest side, near Pike," Jamal said.

"Did you tell him anything?" Corey watched Jamal.

"No. I just told him that the connect was no good. A small timer. JT wants nothing to do with the paperless," Jamal stated.

"Where's the card Tennessee gave you?" Corey asked.

Jamal picked up the card from the coffee table and handed it to Corey.

"What are we going to do?" Mia asked.

"Well, we're not going to Cali. That's off the table," Corey said.

Mia didn't respond. Her faced showed contemplation and that annoyed Corey. He didn't want her to even consider the option of leaving Indy for some mission that would certainly end badly.

"I think we should go." Mia looked at Corey.

"Baby, you've lost your mind? We can't jeopardize our family. Nothing good can come from this." Corey pointed toward the kids' rooms.

"We'll jeopardize them by not going. I can't put my children in danger," Mia admitted.

Corey watched his wife pace back and forth across the room. The weight of her thoughts pressed him.

"We're not going. What do you expect will happen when you get there? When you're done? What do you think payment will be? What wages will you get in return? You'll die out there. Death will be your repayment," Corey said.

"Really? I mean, what could you possibly tell Tennessee about me not going? Or how about we just march down to the police station and let them know that we're being threatened by a guy who runs the west coast. Then let the detectives know that we know him because I used to launder money for you and your father. And then let them know that we may be in connection to possibly two disappearances because we haven't seen or heard from Adrian or Sean in years." Mia's voice cracked

Anger bore a hole into Corey. He didn't want to think of Adrian or his brother. The last he'd heard of them, they were still at it. The blessing was that his family hadn't come looking for him. His prayer had been answered—to be set free and not to be held hostage to the sins of his past. Going back was not an option because returning would be a one-way ticket in reliving a nightmare.

"Mia, go to bed." Corey's threatening calm pierced the quiet room.

"Excuse me?" Mia put both hands on her hips with her head cocked to one side.

"You heard me. You've lost your mind. You need rest. So, go to bed," Corey responded.

"You're right. I'm going to bed. My bed. Don't even think about coming upstairs. Sleep on the couch." Mia quickly walked away, but not before Corey saw the storm in her eyes.

"Look, man. I'm sorry but think about this. If you do go to Cali, it's money involved. This may be a way to get a quick payout. Y'all could be set for a while," Jamal said.

"Get the hell out my house. Don't come back," Corey fumed.

Surrendering, Jamal threw his hands in the air before leaving the house.

"I can't believe this." Corey managed to push away tears of

frustration. He couldn't let them fall.

He was broke with no benefits and a millionaire wanted to employ his pregnant wife. Tennessee would never let her go. Mia was too smart. She'd make felonious money legitimate by any means necessary. He'd been a witness to that.

Fear wiggled its way into his thoughts. Tennessee would not take no for an answer. Corey looked at the card. He would have to give Tennessee a call one way or another.

Chapter Six

Do not say, "I will do to him as he has done to me; I will pay the man back for what he has done." PROVERBS 24:29 ESV

MELODY sat on Amelia's antique chaise and watched her mother-in-law rest in a drug induced sleep. There was no doubt that Amelia was abusing the script. Amelia's dependence on sleep aids and anxiety meds caused the pills to run thin soon after a refill. Amelia appeared frail. Her folded arms made her look like a small, middle school girl. A thick quilt swallowed her, and it barely moved due to her shallow breathing. The woman who had caused Melody extreme grief nearly a year ago was now a victim to her own doing. Amelia's daughter, Peyton, lost her life because she had been ignored. Her pain and suffering had been swept under a rug by her parents in order to preserve their daughter's poster child image for the world. Peyton's face would have easily sat on any red, white, and blue poster with the bold words of: God Bless America.

LAPD labeled Peyton's death as a homicide. There was no lead in her horrific murder. Two bullet holes had pierced her lung. One bullet exited her back and the other lay lodged in the organ's soft tissue. The coroner report revealed her painful death was due to onset respiratory ailure known as hemopneumothorax. The offensive medical term—which the entire Deen family, including Melody, had no clue to the meaning—was hard to digest. When explained in layman's terms it was painful to imagine. Once Peyton was shot, the burning bullets instantly bore holes into her lung. The injured organ filled with blood and air causing it to collapse. She suffocated in her body fluid.

Melody remembered Peyton's beauty. Never had Peyton revealed her pain to her. She wished she had. Maybe Melody could have convinced her not to go to Los Angeles with some nut she'd met online. There was no proof that Peyton's boyfriend, Andrew, had killed her, but a smart person would believe that he was the one.

Now her new family lay torn and stagnant in sorrow and disbelief. Gloom lurked in every corner of the house, squeezing out the bit of life that remained.

"Hey, daughter," Charles Deen said as he stepped in the doorway of Amelia's room.

"Hi." Melody smiled and looked at her tired father-in-law.

"Are you okay?" Charles asked.

"Of course. Just watching Amelia. Making sure she is okay. You know," Melody returned.

"Thank you for this." Charles looked at his wife.

"You know, you don't have to thank me every day," Melody countered.

"Yes, I do. My wife and I were once horrible to you."

"All is forgiven. You both had your reasons," Melody said.

"Reasons that were ridiculous. Now, here we are in need of you." A small, pitiful smile rested on Charles' face.

"I'm glad to help." Melody wondered if she was really glad. She preferred to be in her condo resting in the arms of her husband.

"We thought we were above you. God has a way of turning things around. Now, we are taking a dose of humility," Charles said.

"Yeah." Melody wasn't sure what to say.

"I lost my daughter to my own negligence. I can't ever get her back. Now my wife is dead to the world. She can't even function because of this." Charles' voice cracked.

"Charles, you don't have to do this," Melody said.

"I can't even preach the word to my church because I feel like a hypocrite. I can't tell the people that ministry starts in the home when I didn't start in mine. I can't even talk about forgiveness when I can't forgive the heathen that took my daughter's life," Charles said.

"It's kind of hard to forgive a faceless killer, Charles." Melody tried to find words to cool the atmosphere.

"No, I know who killed her," Charles said.

"I mean we can speculate, but there is no evidence," Melody responded.

"Yeah, well I had evidence. I've had it for a while," Charles admitted.

"What? What do you mean, you had evidence?" Melody couldn't believe what she was hearing.

"I had the evidence. I destroyed it. Pictures of Andrew having Peyton's body removed from the crime scene. I kept a PI on Peyton after Tyler and I left L.A.," Charles said.

"What? Why would you destroy the pictures?" Melody stood.

"I lost my daughter. I've lost my wife to depression. I can't afford to lose my son. If Tyler knows who killed his sister, he will stop at nothing to obtain justice. He's willing to risk everything," Charles said.

"I don't think Tyler will put a bullet in Andrew's head, Charles. You should've taken this evidence to the police. You should've told Tyler. I'm the one living with a man who is not at peace trying to find out about the demise of his sister," Melody said.

"You're missing the picture. If Tyler's focus in on bringing some scumbag to justice, he can't focus on the church. I can't be the pastor of Green Pastures right now. I have to take care of my wife. I can't lose Tyler. He needs to focus on the church, not a millionaire who has enough money to buy his innocence," Charles said.

"Charles, I can't believe this. I hope you don't think I'm not going to tell my husband," Melody said.

"I don't think you will," Charles responded.

"Why is that? Please enlighten me." Melody was livid.

"Think about it. You tell Tyler. He gets mad at me and then loses focus in trying to obtain more evidence to put Andrew under the rug. The family you want won't happen. The time you want with him won't happen. We'll lose him, too, either to his relentless vengeance or due to Andrew killing him," Charles said.

"How do you know about me wanting a family?" Melody was flabbergasted by Charles' intrusiveness.

"It's my job to know," Charles said.

There was nothing left to say. Charles had very valid points.

Tyler sat in his study seething. If anger were a comrade, it would be Tyler's best friend. He hadn't meant to snoop. It was his intention to ask his wife if she needed anything. Melody had spent so much time in the room with Amelia, he wondered if she would ever come back to the guest house. After rounding the corner, he had overheard his father and wife talking. Just as he was going to excuse himself into the room, he heard his father talking about Peyton. Tyler had thought about coming back to Amelia's room as Charles exposed his grief. Then the mention of his father destroying evidence stopped him in his tracks. The great Charles Deen knew of Peyton's killer.

Never a violent man, Tyler resisted the urge to hit his father as he questioned the old man's thinking. How could Charles have done this for the sake of preserving the church? That was the problem. His father always put the church before family. Even after Peyton had been put six feet under, Charles put the church above family by not revealing Peyton's mental instability.

It was time to payback Andrew for what he'd done to this family. Picking up his phone, Tyler scrolled through the contacts. He stopped at one name in particular and pushed the Call icon. It didn't take long for an answer.

"Hello," a light accent answered.

"Aunt Brandy?" Tyler responded.

"Hello nephew. How are you?" Brandy's cheerful voice did nothing to appease Tyler.

"I'm not so good. I…" Tyler felt weakened as he thought of his father's betrayal.

"Tyler, are you okay?" Brandy questioned.

"I'm mad as hell." Tyler couldn't hold his anger back any longer.

"You have a right to be. Your family has been through a lot in the past months," Brandy responded.

"Yeah, I know. Look, I want to get straight to the point," Tyler said.

"Hmmm, A man after my own heart. Go ahead," Brandy said.

"I need you to come to Chicago and look after your sister. I know it's a bit much to ask, but I need my wife to get a break from watching after my mother day and night. And I need you to look after Lena for a bit." Tyler sighed.

"I won't lie, that is a bit much to ask of me. Amelia and I haven't seen each other in years. We only spoke briefly right before Peyton died," Brandy said.

"Was it an amicably conversation?" Tyler asked.

"Very much so. We made plans to meet up, but of course that didn't happen due to unforeseen circumstances," Brandy admitted.

"That's good enough. My mother is incapable of taking care of herself. She is drowning herself in pills after this. My father is…well, let's just say he's dealing with this in his own way." Tyler's frustration was evident.

"Okay, if I agree to this, how receptive will your mother and father be of me? I mean are they able to co-exist with people of natural darker hue?" Brandy laughed to make light of the situation. She remembered her father's secret relationship with her black mother and how much it hurt Amelia to discover his adultery.

"If by that you mean, can they live with a black person under the same roof, the answer is yes. Remember, my wife is African American, and my parents are fine with her," Tyler said.

"Yes, but we both know they gave her pure hell in the beginning. Melody's a strong, reserved woman. I have less restraint. I won't deal to kindly with racist foolishness." Brandy huffed.

"I need you here. I can't do this alone. I have no one else to ask." Tyler sighed.

"When do you want me there?" Brandy asked.

"The sooner the better," Tyler said.

"I'll be there tomorrow night. I'll leave first thing in the morning," Brandy said.

"You're driving?" Tyler asked.

"Yes. I like my feet planted on solid ground, love, not airborne. I'll see you soon. I'll call you when I'm close. Let your folks know I'll be there. I'm not too keen on surprising folks," Brandy said.

"Okay," Tyler said.

"Okay." Brandy hung up the phone.

Tyler was thankful for Brandy's acceptance. Now, he had one more thing left to do. He called his travel agent.

"Hey, Tyler Deen. Glad to hear from you." Tyler's agent picked up the phone rather quickly.

"Hi, Gary." Tyler smiled.

"What can I do for you?"

"I need two tickets to Los Angeles, first class," Tyler responded.

"When?"

"A red eye tomorrow night," Tyler said

"Roundtrip?"

"No," Tyler said.

"Okay. Names on the ticket?"

"Myself and my wife, Melody Deen," Tyler responded.

"Okay, give me half an hour and I'll email you some options. Sound good?"

"Yes." Tyler hung up the phone.

Leaning back in his chair, Tyler wondered how he was going to tell Melody that they were going to avenge Peyton by traveling to Los Angeles. He couldn't leave her behind. He'd hurt her enough by putting their marriage on the back burner while he ran around town late at night trying to obtain fruitless evidence. So, she would have to come with him.

"What are you doing?" Melody interrupted Tyler's thoughts.

"Baby?" Tyler stood to his feet.

"Who were you on the phone with?" Melody asked.

"Gary," he responded.

"Why?" Melody's eyebrows arched in her questioning.

"L.A.," Tyler said.

Staring at Tyler for what felt like eons, Melody finally responded, "Okay."

Chapter Seven

For what does it profit a man to gain the whole world and forfeit his soul? MARK 8:36 ESV

WEARING a pair of vintage aviator glasses, Corey tried to be non-descript in the luxury hotel that sat in the middle of downtown. He decided against wearing jeans and a shirt and instead donned a grey, slim fit, half canvas suit to fit in with the other high paid young business men that frequented the hotel's bustling bistro during lunchtime.

Corey couldn't help but to feel envious as he peeped the millennials merrily eating. This used to be him a few short months ago. Now, he was faking the great life. His last hundred dollars rest in his billfold and by looking at the prices on the menu, a portion of it would go to the cost of eating at such a posh place.

"Have you decided on what you'd like today?" a red head waitress asked Corey.

"I'll take another lemon and water," Corey said, hoping that she wouldn't become annoyed with his delay in making a decision.

"Um, well, okay. I'll be back in a few more minutes to take your order." The waitress was a bit anxious. Corey assumed she was worried about not making a few dollars because he had yet to order food.

Looking around the restaurant again, he spotted a familiar face walking toward him. And his stomach plummeted. Tennessee eased his way through the crowd. The man was still impeccable. His hand stitched suit draped his body like a canvas.

"Corey, I'm so glad you called." Tennessee sat down at the table.

"I had little choice," Corey responded.

"True, and so here we are." Tennessee smiled. "Good selection. Very clean."

"I've enjoyed eating here from time to time," Corey said.

Nodding his head in approval, Tennessee took one more look of his surroundings then placed his full attention on Corey. "How's the domestic life treating you?"

"Couldn't be better," Corey lied. Right now, Mia was barely speaking to him.

"Hmmm, you don't sound too convincing. I'm guessing the money is a little harder to get." Tennessee smirked.

"I'm managing," Corey said.

Opening his suit jacket, Tennessee pulled out two white envelopes. He handed one to Corey.

"What is this?" Corey asked.

"Open it." Tennessee gestured.

Corey opened the envelope and pulled out a few sheets of paper. After scanning the documents, his blood pressure rose instantaneously. How had Tennessee gotten his current bank statement? The balance was written in bold letters—$5.18. A copy of his employment termination letter was behind the statement.

"Don't insult me with your questions of how. You already know who I am. If I have to remind you, then refer to me as all knowing. Something like the invisible god you serve," Tennessee said as his attention was pulled to the redhead waitress standing in front of them.

"Hello, my name is Mandy and I—"

The poor girl was interrupted by Tennessee. "Here's a little something for you. If we're still here in twenty minutes, come back and I'll slide you a bit more, but do leave us alone." Tennessee pushed a one-hundred-dollar bill across the table to the young woman.

Mandy peered at the money for a few seconds, tucked it in her bra, and walked away.

"She's smart. She's going places." Tennessee smiled.

"Why are you showing me this?" Corey pointed to the envelope.

Tennessee handed Corey the second envelope.

After reading its contents, Corey's pulse once again quickened. The last time he had access to that many zeros was back in California.

"That's my offer. Your wife does this one thing for me, I let her come back home," Tennessee said.

"Even if we agreed to this absurd offer, I wouldn't let her go alone," Corey said.

"You can come with her. It could very much be like a couple's getaway for a week or two. She'll work during the day and you both can have the evenings together. It'll be all expensed paid. I have a beautifully renovated home right off Santa Monica. It'll be yours during your stay. You might want to stay once you get a taste of the good life again. I'll give you the place. It'll be like a coming back home present." Tennessee leered.

"What if we say no?" Corey asked.

"Jamal should've informed you," Tennessee said.

"Enlighten me again," Corey countered.

"I thought we would be able to keep this conversation civil, but I guess I underestimated your drive to be a better man. Bottom line, you know my capabilities. I can't keep trying to prove myself to you. You know this. I know where you live. I know where you used to work. I know your wife is pregnant. I know how much you love CJ and Taylor. And I know you're living hand to mouth and your beautiful wife doesn't even know it. Let's cut the bull, Corey." Tennessee appeared a bit irritated at Corey's questioning.

Corey swallowed. Tennessee hadn't given him much choice. The threat against his family was imminent. The risk of him being late on the next mortgage payment was imminent, too. The pressure was overwhelming. God brought him out the last time, but this time a lot more people were involved, and Corey's faith was teetering. Mia was all ready to go. She was practically waiting on him. They would be going backward. What God had once delivered them from, they were returning to in doubt and fear.

"When do you want us there?" Corey couldn't believe he was giving in to this outrageous request. The consequences of money laundering were numerous.

"I've tickets for you two tomorrow. First class." Tennessee pulled yet another envelope from his jacket and handed it to Corey.

"Yeah, thanks," Corey said and stood.

Taking the envelope, Corey nodded his head toward a thoroughly satisfied Tennessee and walked from the restaurant. He'd sold his soul, his wife's soul, and children's souls to the devil and now he would forever reap the consequences of his actions.

As he held back tears of self-pity and pain, he managed to walk a few blocks toward the city's neoclassical monument. Ironically, the landmark honored the brave, fallen soldiers of wars past, and he stood by the statue of bravery as a coward.

The crowds of people soon became moving blurs as Corey sat on a bench. He needed help. God was nowhere in his decision to go to Cali, so he held back a prayer. Instead, he pulled his phone from his pocket and scrolled through his contacts. He dreaded the name he was searching for but knew there was little choice. Wondering if it still worked, he pushed the Call button.

"Yeah?" A deep voice connected with Corey's ear.

"Dad?" Corey asked.

"Corey?" Adrian responded.

"Yes."

"Why are you calling me? You're dead to me. Remember? You chose tail over an empire."

"I chose God." Corey wondered if his own declaration were true.

"Really? Are you sure? Because you're calling me."

"I need your help," Corey murmured.

"What the hell? I know I didn't hear you say you needed something from me. Please, boy!"

"My family is being threatened, man." Corey felt wetness penetrate his eyes.

Silence passed through the line as both men thought.

Adrian voice softened. "It's a part of the game. It's not fair, but it's the enemy's job to know where it hurts."

"I even have one on the way," Corey said.

"Who's the threat?"

"Tennessee."

Corey could hear several vulgar curses through the phone.

"What do you need me to do, son?" Adrian asked.

"Protection for my family."

"Count it done."

"Mia and I will be there tomorrow night."

"Call me as soon as your plane lands to give me your location," Adrian responded.

'Thank you." Corey hung up the phone.

Corey pulled out the tickets to see their exact departure and thirty crisp one hundred-dollar bills sat in the envelope. A note was attached.

Pay your bills. It's more where this came from. You will gain the world for a small price.

Chapter Eight

For we do not wrestle against flesh and blood, but against the rulers, against the authorities, against the cosmic powers over this present darkness, against the spiritual forces of evil in the heavenly places. EPHESIANS 6:12 ESV

TYLER sat in the living room of the Deen estate watching Lena play with her toys. His 3-year-old daughter was fascinating. Watching her grow into a curious little girl was an amazing journey. Lena looked like a small replica of her mother—beautiful, smooth, brown skin; large, bright eyes; and head of hair that coiled past her shoulders. He wondered how Edward could just abandon such a gift, but in secret Tyler was somewhat satisfied that baby daddy wasn't in the picture. The last time he and Melody saw the man, he was a mess. Edward had practically committed mental suicide in a one room efficiency apartment. The halfway house in which he stayed housed a depressed motley crew.

From what Tyler heard, Edward had gone to a few counseling sessions to seek help for himself, but eventually stopped going. The guy's parents grew tired of him staying at the family home without a job and put him out. Melody wanted Lena to have a relationship with her biological father, but after she heard rumors of him drinking and filling the pockets of prostitutes with his monthly disability check, she ceased the issue.

Little Lena now called Tyler "Dad" and he had no problem with it.

"Daddy, where is Mommy?" Lena walked over to Tyler.

"She's at home," Tyler responded as he picked her up and placed her on his knee.

"Why are we not at home?" Lena asked.

"Because Mommy is taking a break." Tyler smiled thinking of how Melody looked so peaceful while sleeping.

"A break? Why does she need a break?" Lena asked another question.

Tyler was intrigued by her consistent inquisitiveness.

"Sometimes mommies and daddies just need a break, sweetheart. We need rest, too," Tyler said.

Lena's large eyes smiled at her father for a while. Finally, she shrugged her shoulders and walked toward her stuffed animals to pour them tea. Tyler was happy that she did. He wasn't ready to explain to her that her mother was finishing up the packing and that they would soon be leaving her in the care of relatives.

Tyler and Melody momentarily thought of taking Lena with them, but after a short consideration, they had decided against it. Putting their daughter in harm's way would not be wise. Tyler wondered if they made the right choice to leave her with his parents, aunt, and the housekeeper. Amelia was barely stable, and Charles was consumed in church preservation. So that meant Lena would have to lean on a stranger and the housekeeper. Guilt bore a hole through him. He was so adamant about avenging his sister, he forgot about the wellbeing of his daughter. Looking heavenward, he asked God to put a hedge around Lena as he tried to make sense of the craziness that hit the family like a ton of bricks.

"Son?" Amelia walked slowly into the room.

Tyler assessed his mother. Her once perfectly coifed tresses were now long and unkempt. Gone was the golden bob that shaved years from her age. In its place where shapeless strings of hair. Pale white skin covered her thin body and the chalkiness of her hue contrasted with the dark circles around her eyes. She looked twenty years older than her actual age.

"Mom, you should be in bed," Tyler said.

"You're probably right, but what good will it do? I need a change of scenery." Amelia talked through chapped lips.

"Are you hungry?" Tyler asked even though he knew her answer.

"No," Amelia said as she watched Lena pour make believe tea into a cup. A small smile breached her face.

"Dad tell you about Melody and me?" Tyler was careful of his words. He didn't want to alarm Lena of her parents' departure.

"Yes, he did. Said that you all were taking an impromptu trip to New York for a week or so," Amelia said.

"Yes, we just need a getaway. Melody needs some time away. She's stressed." Tyler partially lied. They were definitely not going to New York, but his wife needed a break.

"And you are leaving Lena?" Amelia asked.

"Is that a problem?" Tyler countered.

"Absolutely not. It will be good to have a ball of energy run through the house. She might give me a little life," Amelia said as she looked at Lena. "Peyton used to have a similar tea set. She served tea to her stuffed animals, too."

Tyler could hear the familiar pain in his mother's voice as she wrestled with her daughter's dark past. The driving knife of agony was all too recognizable.

"You'll have a guest to help take care of her." Tyler was ready to talk about Brandy.

"Well, if you consider Darrya guest, then I guess," Amelia said.

"No," Tyler responded.

"No?" Amelia queried.

"It's Brandy. She'll be here soon," Tyler said.

"I don't think I'm ready to see her. This is not a good time." Amelia pulled her long sweater close to her chest.

"This is the perfect time. My wife is on the brink of a meltdown in this house of horrors... I mean in this place." Tyler regretted his reference to the family home although true.

Amelia sighed. "I haven't seen her in years."

"This is a good time as any. She's full of love and energy. She's perfect for what you and Dad need now." Tyler wanted to sell the case and be able to leave, regret free, in a few short hours.

"Alright. I'll try," Amelia quietly said.

Tyler wondered if the 15 milligrams of Aripiprazole had an effect on her friction free response, but he had no time to consider as the doorbell rang.

"I believe she is here," Tyler said as he waited for Darrya to answer the door.

A brief greeting was heard before footsteps made their way through the grand foyer to the parlor. Tyler stood when his aunt entered the room. She grinned as he looked at the darker version of his mother. Brandy put her arms around Tyler and he returned the embrace.

"Nephew, it's good to see you again," Brandy said.

"Aunt, you look great," Tyler said as he stepped back.

Brandy smiled at a standing Amelia. Both sisters stood quietly as they regarded one another. Tyler held his breath. This had to work. He'd taken a risk when he called Brandy, but his mother needed something or someone. She'd become quite attached to Melody, but his wife was for him.

Brandy moved first, and Amelia followed. Both sisters wrapped their arms around one another and cried. This was Tyler's cue to pick up Lena and leave. She didn't hesitate to jump into his arms. He gathered she didn't want to be around to hear a lot of loud crying. They went home to eat a meal before he left his baby girl in what he hoped would be an amicable reunion.

"Ladies and gentlemen, the caption has turned on the fasten seat belt sign. If you haven't already done so, please put your carry-on luggage in an overhead compartment. Please take your seat and fasten your seat belt. Also, make sure your seat and folding trays are in a full upright position."

The assigned flight attendant read the script in preparation for takeoff. Tyler sat by the window and watched the lights shining on the ground.

"Are we going to be okay?" Melody asked Tyler as she fastened her seatbelt.

"Yes, baby. We'll be fine. No need to worry," Tyler responded as he patted his wife's hand.

Melody didn't really like to fly. She tolerated it, but if there was a way to avoid the friendly skies, she'd much rather choose that option.

"I'm not talking about the flight. Well, at least not really. I'm talking about us going on this vigilante trip as imposter detectives," Melody said.

Tyler's eyebrows quirked in response to Melody's description of their travels. He wasn't sure that they would become some rogue vigilantes, but he needed answers.

"Baby, we're going to be fine. I just need to meet with a few people about Peyton. I will be nowhere near Andrew. Once the meeting is over, we'll take in the sights, or we can take in each other." Tyler grinned.

Melody blushed, but soon her serious face returned. "Do you promise this meeting will be safe?"

Tyler couldn't lie to his wife. He wrestled with his own thoughts of whether or not his fight for Peyton's justice was for his sister or with a more sinister power. It was more of faith versus fury that trapped his mind from day to day.

The truth was that he would be alone when he met with his connect. Not wanting to alarm Melody, he answered the question without answering the question.

"When we meet, it will be brief. You'll be safe. I love you, woman." Tyler squeezed his wife's hand.

"Cabin Crew, prepare for gate departure. Flight attendants, doors are on automatic, cross-check and report. Thank you."

The captain's voice was clear as it came through the speaker. This was it. There was no turning back now. He'd soon be fighting against wickedness in high places. In four hours and thirty minutes, they would be arriving at LAX. The cabin air recirculating through the vents filled Tyler's nostrils, stopping him from taking in a deep breath. Instead, he blew out a tired breath.

"You know, I'm only doing this because I love you, right?" Melody said.

"Of course. You know, baby, you can always take a turn around flight when we get to L.A. I don't want you to feel obligated to go with me," Tyler admitted.

"Well, for one, I can't let you do this alone. I need you back in one piece. I don't think I can make it as a widow or wife of a man doing life. It would break my heart. Second, I'm not riding a plane by myself for over four hours. No way. No how," Melody said.

"And you won't," Tyler said.

Melody's free hand gripped the arm rest of the seat. The extra hundreds of dollars he'd paid for first class did nothing to ease her anxiety. The first time they'd ridden a plane together, Melody nearly passed out from the turbulence. He wondered why she hadn't gotten over her fear as they were on a plane every other month. Rubbing her back, he smiled to reassure her that all was well.

"Flight attendants, prepare for take-off, please. We are next in line for departure."

Soon, the roar of the engines sounded as the jet accelerated down the runway. A slight vibration could be felt as the massive plane rolled. Within moments, the nose of the plane tilted and ascended into the sky. Melody closed her eyes and her lips quietly moved. Tyler knew she was praying. He popped his earbuds in his ears and tried to take a nap. His wife didn't talk much on the plane due to her nervousness. He was certain she would be in a vegetative trance until the plane landed.

As the couple drifted into their own world, they were oblivious to a seething Kelly watching them from two rows behind. Her hair was tucked deeply into a baseball cap and her eyes hid behind large shades. She was unsure why her boyfriend wanted her to follow her ex, but he'd been adamant, and she was not at liberty to disappoint. It had been torturous to watch what could have been her husband cling to Melody.

She wished she could at least send a message to her man, but her phone was on airplane mode. She wouldn't be able to do anything until she landed.

"Well, Andrew, I'll talk to you later," Kelly whispered to herself.

She took one last look at Tyler, closed her eyes, and imagined what life would have been like if she were the First Lady of Green Pastures.

Chapter Nine

But each person is tempted when he is lured and enticed by his own desire. JAMES 1:14 ESV

COREY felt a sense of panic when he noticed his sister-in-law and her husband waiting at the baggage claim in the bustling LAX airport. Mia was too busy looking for their luggage and hadn't yet noticed their presence. At any other time, Corey would've whistled across the crowd to get his family's attention, but under the current circumstances he was preparing to duck behind a stranger.

He did wonder why Melody and Tyler had not mentioned they would be in Los Angeles, but they could say the same.

"Corey, what are you doing?" Mia asked as Corey stilled her movements

"We have to go. Now," Corey said.

"Yes, we do." Mia's eyes followed Corey's and rested on her sister.

Corey grabbed their luggage, and they quickly headed toward the terminal curbside. The busyness of the airport was sheer madness. It was organized chaos at best. Weeding through the crowd, Corey nearly pulled his wife to gain distance from Melody and Tyler.

"Dude, watch out," a sour faced, middle aged man said as Corey nearly knocked him down.

"I'm sorry, man. I wasn't paying attention," Corey responded.

"I know. You almost knocked me down!" The man's rancid breath blared from his mouth and bounced in Corey's nose.

"I said I'm sorry, man. I just didn't see you," Corey said.

"And I said, you blind idiot, that you almost knocked me down. Watch out and pay attention. You in L.A. now. Keep your eyes open!"

Corey gently pulled his wife behind him and her hand went to his shoulder. "You don't know who I am. So, I'm going to let you slide. Talk to me like that again and I'm going to break your jaw." Corey's jaw pulsed. He hadn't meant to become indignant, but the pressure of his in-laws spotting him pushed his adrenaline.

"Alright, man." The man's voice became a bit quieter as he backed away with hands in the air.

"Don't disrespect me—" Corey started but was interrupted by Mia.

"Corey, stop. What are you doing?" Mia searched Corey's face. "This is not you. Let's go."

Corey stepped away from the man, gripped Mia's hand, and continued through the crowd. His heart drummed in his chest. Mia was right. What was he doing? He hadn't been back in L.A. for no more than half an hour and he was back at his old ways of intimidating people. He needed air.

"Corey? Slowdown. Why are we running? I'm pretty sure Melody and Tyler don't see us." Mia pulled his hand.

"I'm sorry, baby. I'm just tired. I need to get out of here." Fear of the unknown rattled him. "There is no good to come from us being here," Corey said.

His thoughts shifted back to the man. He was about to tell the guy that he was Phillips Cartel for life, baby, and then he remembered God had delivered him. The thought of busting guns, popping bands on rolled bills, and checking weight made him break into a sweat.

"Are you having second thoughts?" Mia was now in a light trot with her husband.

"No, I just need some air," Corey said.

"It's okay, baby. I'm scared, too." Mia tried to slow her steps, but Corey was adamant in his hasty exit.

"Mia, Let's go." Frustration got the best of him.

No!" Mia stopped.

"What are you doing?" Corey looked at Mia and back to where his in-laws were once standing. They were gone.

"Apparently, I'm about to have an argument with my husband in one of the busiest airports in the world." Mia frowned. "I don't even care because I'm not about to be pulled like a toddler on a rope."

"Look, we have to go. We have a deadline. We don't have time for a tantrum."

"Okay, but do you have time for me to lose this baby? My feet hurt. My pelvis is aching, and I haven't had anything decent to eat in over four hours. So, excuse me if I don't become an Olympiad up in here." Mia's voice cranked up a notch causing a few people to stare.

Looking at his wife, Corey saw a face that reflected exactly what he was feeling—fear. He needed to deescalate the situation.

Corey got on one knee and turned his back to Mia. "Get on."

"What are you doing?" Mia looked around.

"Hooking up my best friend. Come on." Corey patted his back.

"Are you serious?" Mia tried to cover her smile.

"I'm so serious. The next time your feet touch the ground, we'll be standing in front of some food," Corey said as he leaned in to kiss her stomach.

"Okay. I love you, Corey." Mia smiled as she got on his back.

"We're in this together. We're going to get through this," Corey said.

"Corey, I'm worried about the kids," Mia whispered in his ear.

"You mom and dad are looking after them. They are in the best hands possible," Corey responded.

"What if something happens?" Mia wrapped her arms tighter around him.

"We can't think like that." Corey stood and adjusted to the weight of his wife on his back. Grabbing the suitcase, he maneuvered through the crowd.

Tennessee spared no expense on his luxurious beachfront home. Each piece of furniture appeared to be selected from some upscale store only open to the elite. This place reminded Corey of the life he once knew that afforded him freedom to take care of himself. He missed that.

Corey walked into the large, open space of the living room and looked out the floor to ceiling window onto the beach. God created such wonder—the water, sun, and even the birds that seemed to fly into the horizon, yet He also allowed this chaos to infiltrate his life once again.

Money and power came hand in hand like a bride and groom. He left a life of poverty as a child to live with his father, the king of the Phillips cartel. With the hunger for money, they became powerful. He'd been tempted with his personal desire for the need to push past the level of basic living. His need came with such a high price. He'd lost people dear to him and he nearly lost his soul.

Corey glanced at his sleeping wife. She was only in the first trimester of pregnancy and he'd read that this was the most critical time for the baby. The embryo was most vulnerable to damage at this stage. They were in the eye of the hurricane. If it came to it, he would take the blame and go to prison for the sake of his family. Never would he allow his wife to sit in some six-by-eight foot cell for years. Ultimately, all this mess was his fault. Had he never taken her to California three years ago, she wouldn't have met these awful people.

A flickering light could be seen outside the window by the shore. It moved for his muse as he moved closer to take a better look. Squinting, he noticed a figure signaling him to come out. He glanced at a peaceful Mia. He knew she'd be sleep for at least another hour. He grabbed his phone, exited, and headed towards the person who was now waiting for him.

As he approached, familiarity hit him. Relief and anger coursed through him as he saw his father. He knew his father was a powerful man. So finding where they were staying had been no problem.

"Adrian?" Corey asked.

"Son." Adrian's eyes traveled over him.

Adrian hadn't changed much. Salt and pepper hair was still cut close and his piercing eyes were still mad.

"I'm glad to see that you are…" Corey couldn't finish his thoughts.

"You're glad to see that your old man isn't six feet under or sitting in a jail cell. Right? Yeah, well me, too. But trust, when you left I had one foot in the grave." Adrian snorted.

"I never wanted to see you hurt. I just wanted out." Corey was honest.

"Yet, here you are with the woman that helped start this whole mess," Adrian said.

"I need your help." Corey ignored his father's jab at Mia.

"Fate has a funny way of turning things around. You screwed me over and now life's screwing you."

"Why are you here? If you're so mad about me leaving, then why even bother? I don't have time for this." Corey started to walk away. Maybe contacting Adrian had been a mistake.

"Wait!" Adrian held Corey's arm. "Look, I ain't going to lie. I made an empire for you and you just walked away. That's disloyal, but you're my blood. My seed. You have a wife and family. I can't let harm come your way. To do that would go against honor. I lost Keith. I can't lose you, too."

"Where's Sean?" Corey wondered about his brother.

"Serving a three-year sentence in state. Caught a felony last March for possession with intent to sell. Three grams of that nose candy. That's no time. The FEDs said they would drop the charges if he gave them a few names. Sean put his fists out and told them boys good luck. That's a warrior!" Adrian boastfully hit his chest.

"Do you see him?" Corey asked.

"Naw, man. I can't visit him. They want me in a jail cell right next to Sean, but I do send someone twice a month to talk with him for me and I keep money on his books. He don't want for nothing. That's for sure," Adrian said.

"Okay," Corey said.

"So, tell me, what's going on with you?"

"Tennessee wants Mia to set up shop for some connect. Something similar to what we had a few years ago. Quick in and out. Then we leave. Go back to our lives," Corey said.

"You've really gotten dumb. Tennessee ain't going to let her go back. And you're the icing on the cake. You won't leave her. So, he'll be able to recruit one of Cali's finest soldiers. He'll convince you to permanently come out of retirement. He's thought this through and through, son," Adrian said.

"He said two weeks." Corey's admittance sounded weak to his own ears.

"Yeah, two weeks until the honeymoon period is dead and you and your missus will be property of Tennessee, LLC, man," Adrian said.

"We had no choice," Corey stated.

"You're right. You didn't."

"So, what do I do?"

"Be smart. Don't ask any questions. Do your job. I'll get back to you soon."

"When?" Corey needed a more definite time.

"It is not your job to know of the times or seasons that I have fixed by my own authority." Adrian winked his eye.

"I see you've been reading the bible, but you're not God." Corey smiled.

"Yeah, I've been doing lots of things you wouldn't know about since you've been gone. And right now, God ain't helping you. I'll talk with you soon," Adrian said before walking away.

Corey watched his father walk into the distance. Breathing deeply, he could taste the salt of the sea on the back of his tongue and it reminded him once again the carefree life that he used to have. He and his brothers used to have weekend parties on the beach that lasted days. They were epic all-nighters and meant the cartel had just scored a lot of money. Corey smiled. He missed being with his brothers, but there was no turning back. Or was it? Temptation lurked and pushed for a breakthrough.

Chapter Ten

... but envy makes the bones rot. Proverbs 14:30 ESV

Edward lay in the bed of his studio apartment staring at a bottle of amber colored liquor sitting on the nightstand. It was nearly empty, and he still wanted more of the warm drink that felt good going down. It was even better at helping him deal with the pain of his past. Years went by and he still missed his wife, Mia. Many believed time healed all wounds, but Edward's situation proved to be different. Time had only created an open grave in which he buried his sorrows.

"Hey, where's my money?" A petite woman exited the shower.

Her hair lay damp and wavy around her shoulders giving her a wet and wild look.

Edward didn't even know her name. She was a warm body that barely kept his mind off his wife for a while. She was an easy hired fix that didn't ask questions.

"It's on the chair." Edward pointed while continuing to look at the bottle. He wondered if he could make it to the liquor store and buy some more Cognac before the game came on television.

"You're twenty dollars short." The woman huffed as she slipped on her jogging pants and tank top.

"And you got mad a while ago. I'm not paying for your attitude."

"You kept calling me some chick named Mia."

"Does it matter? I'm paying. I can call you what I want. Now get out."

"Loser! Whoever she is, she'd be smart to leave you." She grabbed the money and stormed from the room. The woman's anger didn't bother him. He was glad that she made a hasty exit. Taking his eyes from the liquor, he stared at an old pic of Mia. She looked so beautiful in a blue dress that hugged her in all the right places. She'd just turned twenty-four and they had celebrated in Miami.

He remembered telling her that they would grow old together. It wasn't true now. She divorced him, sold their dream home, and remarried. She belonged to another man and had even given him a son.

"I could've given you sons," Edward whispered as the envy rotted his bones.

Even though years passed since the dissolution of their marriage, the pain still cut like the day she put the papers on their marital bed for him to sign. He thought, perhaps, over time, she would come to her senses and realize that he'd made a horrible mistake. Six months after their hasty divorce, Mia was walking down the aisle with a self-proclaimed delivered gangster from Los Angeles.

Edward hated Corey for being a better man. Watching Mia blush and smile whenever that man touched her made Edward cringe. She used to smile at him like that. Even hearing his beloved daughter, Taylor, refer to him as Papa, made him ill.

So, since Corey felt so freely to take another man's family, Edward took something from him. Sending an anonymous letter to Corey's job had been epic. The man didn't even know what hit him when the CEO gave him his walking papers. The lack of finances could damage a marriage and Edward was hoping to put an ax in the one belonging to Corey.

The ringing of the phone interrupted his thoughts. Taylor was calling. It wasn't too often that she thought enough to pick up the phone to check on her old man.

"What's up, love?" Edward tried to sound upbeat.

"Oh, nothing. Just checking on you. Letting you know that I miss you," Taylor admitted.

Edward smiled a bit. It was good to know that Taylor stopped hating him. It had taken nearly two years, but she finally loved him again.

"I miss you, too, angel. What are you doing today?" Edward asked.

It was pointless to ask if she wanted to come over and hang out for a while. A few months ago, Melody, his ex-mistress, witnessed his drunkenness and spread the word that he was an alcoholic. After that, the supervised visits for Taylor and his youngest daughter, Lena, stopped.

"I'm pretty much doing nothing. CJ and I are over grandma and grandpa's house for the next few weeks." Taylor sighed.

"Oh, your mom and Corey grew tired of you both and shipped you to the house of spoils?" Edward's curiosity peaked. He hadn't been ready to hear that his wife had gone on a vacation.

"No. We're not spoiled. They had to go to Los Angeles." Taylor laughed.

"California?" Edward thought Mia had vowed to never set foot into that state again. He never knew what exactly happened when Mia ran off for months in Los Angeles after she discovered his infidelity, but it wasn't good. Whatever happened scared her enough to come back to Indianapolis and never speak of her experience in the city of angels.

"Yes, California. I wanted to go, but you know how that goes," Taylor said.

"Yeah." Edward didn't have much to say. He needed to know why Mia and Corey left.

"Well, I guess I'd better go. I'll call you later," Taylor said.

"Yeah, do that," Edward said then hung up the phone.

Edward logged into his account from his phone, checking to see if his disability funds had been deposited. Confirming the payment, he zipped up his jeans, pulled on a shirt, and headed out the door. He needed to talk to Brandon, his therapist, at the mental health center. He didn't have an appointment, but this was somewhat of an emergency. His wife and Corey had left to go to California. What if she moved there? How would he be able to get a chance to reconcile their marriage? How would he be able to touch her smooth caramel skin? How could she be able to have his children so far away?

"Why is she leaving? Why didn't she say anything to me?" Edward mumbled to himself.

He was relieved that his therapist was only a block away. When he was placed in the studio apartment through a recovery program, it was suggested that he be in close proximity to his doctor. At first, he

71

found the recommendation insulting. He was no psycho. He was just trying to pick up the pieces after Mia left. It was just taking him a bit longer to pull it together. That was all.

Just because his behavior was peculiar to many, he was unfairly labeled with onset bi-polar disorder with erotomania. Those big words made him sound crazy. He was just in love with his wife and she was in love with him, too. Corey was just in the way.

He finally made it to the center. He pushed through the line to the front desk.

"Mr. Johnson, how are you today?" The petite, red head receptionist smiled.

"Hi, Madeline. I'm good. Is Brandon available?" Edward smiled hoping his charm would help her ignore his pushiness.

"I'll see, but you know you just stepped in front of a line.' Madeline's sing song voice had been trained to neutralize patients like Edward.

Edward peeked behind him and saw several screwed up faces "Yeah, I didn't mean to do that. I just really need to see Brandon. My wife is in trouble!"

"Have a seat, Mr. Johnson. I'll let Brandon know you are here." Madeline gestured for him to sit down in the waiting area.

Edward grudgingly walked to a seat and stared at the quiet green wall. He felt like a child sent to his room. A few people continued to openly gawk at him because of his bold entry, but he didn't care.

"Mr. Johnson?" It didn't take long for Brandon's nurse to call his name.

Standing, Edward followed the tall man into the office of his therapist. Immediately, Edward sat on the large inviting settee. As he leaned into the seat, he looked at the older man in front of him. The guy was a visual stereotype of a psychologist. Wire rhymed glasses were perched on his nose. A light blue button-down shirt was tucked neatly into khaki pants. Brown leather loafer rested on his feet.

"Hi, Edward," Brandon said.

"Hey, Brandon. Thanks for seeing me," Edward responded.

"No problem. Glad to help. What's going on? I was told it was urgent." Brandon pulled a pen from his shirt pocket.

"It's my wife. She's left to go to California and she didn't tell me," Edward began.

"Why has she gone to California?" Brandon was busy writing on his pad.

"I have no idea. She left with Corey. She can't go to California. Something bad happened to her there."

"Edward, do you remember?" Brandon stopped writing and looked at his client.

"No! I already told you. We've talked about this." Edward's voice became a bit louder.

"Remember, Edward. I want you to think with me. Mia is no longer your wife." Brandon spoke softly.

"She's my wife!" Edward said.

"She was, but she divorced you. Remember? You had an affair with her sister. You have a daughter by Melody," Brandon said.

"Mia will come to her senses. I... I messed up... I..." Edward stammered.

"Edward, did you take your meds?" Brandon frowned.

"No, I..." Edward began to tear up.

"When was the last time you took them?" Brandon put his pen and notepad on his desk to give Edward his full attention.

"Two, maybe three weeks ago. I don't remember." Edward's head fell to his hands.

"I want to have you stay in our residential facility for a few days. Just for observation and get those meds working again, buddy." Brandon pushed the call button on his desk.

"I... `I messed up, man. I'm not married to her anymore. She has a man. She's happy now," Edward cried.

Brandon didn't respond. He was busy speaking with his assistant to prepare a rehabilitative stay for Edward. The therapist's intent was clear. Edward would have a two-week mandatory stay in the state of Indiana's finest governmental subsidized housing for the mentally disabled. Edward had been down this road before. When he didn't take his meds, his mind jerked him back into a past that he desperately wished were true.

"I just want my wife. I want Mia back in my life," Edward whispered as he waited for a team of nurses to escort him to the upstairs facility.

Chapter Eleven

The people dwelling in darkness have seen a great light, and
for those dwelling in the region and shadow of death, on them
a light has dawned. MATTHEW 4:16 ESV

ANDREW leaned back in his chair and watched the monitor. Mia
and Corey talked with one another in Tennessee's home. They
appeared happy and full of light. Somehow, the audio wasn't working
and that disturbed him. He was curious about them, especially the
woman. The stories he'd heard about her skills were no less than
perfect. He was excited to have her as a part of his team. They would
work well together. He was tired of trying to hide his money in offshore accounts while giving up ridiculous percentages of his profits
to keep his earnings off the FEDS grid.

He was scheduled to meet the power couple tonight. They were
a Godly couple at that. And that made the deal much sweeter. It
was always good to see an angel fall back into the realities of this
world. He finessed an angel once until she grew her conscience
back. That turned out to be a shame because he felt something for
Peyton. He had felt something for a few women before her, but they
all turned out to be disappointments that had to be put down like
rabid. A rebound relationship followed, but nothing in comparison
to his beautiful Peyton. A fast groupie by the name of Kelly was now

temporarily by his side. He knew she had connections with the Deen family and that's why he kept the incorrigible woman close. It was not by coincidence that he met her in a Chicago bar not soon after Peyton's funeral. He followed the voluptuous Kelly after spying on the burial of Peyton. He remembered.

Andrew watched from a distance as Tyler and Melody stood over the open grave of Peyton. All were dressed in black. Amelia even wore a black lace veil in mourning of her daughter. The sobbing older woman could barely contain her grief as her husband wrapped his arms around her. A large picture of the golden-haired Peyton sat on a black easel. The picture reminded him of the front cover of a beauty magazine. Peyton's long tresses had been captured blowing in the wind and a wide smile showing perfectly white teeth encased by ruby red lips. He'd tasted the lips, and those lips had tasted parts of him. He shivered thinking of her and briefly became angry when remembering putting two bullets in a perfect body. Just as he was about to turn, he noticed a shapely woman standing near a tree intently watching the family. Her main focus was Tyler who was tossing roses on the top of the casket. Her above the knee black wrap dress hugged every inch of her, and Andrew immediately knew that woman wanted Tyler. Just as Melody wrapped her arms around Tyler, Kelly scowled and walked away. The Deen family was oblivious to the inferno blazing within her. Andrew knew he could get more information about his beloved Peyton from a scorned woman. He never would've imagined the Deen's ties to Mia Phillips.

Lately Kelly's demands for money, time, and monogamy tempted Andrew to put two bullets in her back just like he did Peyton. However, the extreme woman proved to be useful in getting information about the Deen family and she was hell bent in trying to ruin the life of Melody Deen.

Andrew couldn't care less about Kelly's personal vendetta against the woman, but since her grudge was toward the sister of Mia, he had a problem. He needed Mia to be focused about his money, and if Kelly did anything to cause his personal cash cow to worry, then he would unleash his wrath.

"Tyler and Melody are in their hotel." Kelly walked in Andrew's office.

She was wearing one of Peyton's dresses that he'd bought her during his stay in Chicago. It was a tad bit tight, but he figured she liked ultra-fitted clothing.

"Okay," Andrew responded

"You don't seem too surprised." Kelly huffed.

Andrew sighed. "I'm glad that you took it upon yourself to let me know, Kelly. But I knew that already."

"Oh, how could you know?" Kelly asked.

"It's my business to know. Let it be. Did you get my message?" Andrew changed the subject.

"Yes, you want me to somehow get Tyler to notice me?" Kelly rolled her eyes heavenward.

"Is there a problem?" Andrew watched Kelly.

"I mean, Tyler is pretty much done with me after he dumped me for that thing. I mean he is completely in love with that black woman!" Kelly sneered.

"Yeah. I see the problem. It's loud and clear." Andrew's gaze traveled from the top of her head to her feet.

"I'm not a racist if that is what you're thinking," Kelly whined. "I just think for him, he could've been more successful if his little missus was not of the darker persuasion."

"And you're for certain that he could do better with someone… like…perhaps yourself," Andrew said.

"Absolutely." Kelly nodded. "But, I got you now. That's what matters, babe."

"I'm no fan of judging people on the basis of their skin color. The only color that is at the top of my list is the rich color of the green American dollar. That makes the world go 'round, Kelly. I don't care who holds the dollar when it's put into my hands. Dark, black, yellow, red, white… I don't care," Andrew proclaimed.

"What are you trying to say?" Kelly asked.

"What I'm trying to say is that I let nothing get in my way to get money. Why should you let a color stop you? Get some ambition and drive and stop complaining. You came after me as soon as your would-be sister-in-law disappeared. You recognized me in that bar," Andrew said.

"Yes, I remember. I recognized you." Kelly smiled.

Andrew swallowed. He missed Peyton. A small bit of remorse coursed through him.

"So, you're saying I should just go after Tyler with full force…with ambition, huh?" Kelly continued oblivious to Andrew's distress.

"Just remember to come home to Daddy, baby," Andrew lied. She was getting on his nerves.

"Really?" Kelly smiled.

"This is an in and out mission. If Melody sees her man is a cheater. Tyler will be destroyed. He'll have no time to blame me for killing his sister," Andrew said.

"I know. I think it's absurd that he would even think you would do something like that." Kelly shook her head.

"Yeah, that's crazy." Andrew smiled.

"I'm going to make you proud." Kelly beamed.

"I'm sure." Andrew nodded.

"I'll get back with you on my progress." Kelly walked toward the door and blew a kiss.

"See you soon." Andrew was grateful that Kelly left.

Andrew stared at the monitor once again watching Mia and Corey move around the house. It was very entertaining and a reminder of what he used to be. He'd forgotten what ordinary people do and looking at the young couple was like making sense of a fish climbing a tree. Years ago, he was a man looking for a way out of a world full of cut throat people. Andrew was glad to be out of the fish tank, but sometimes he missed the water.

It was time to meet them.

Pulling up to the large tower like building reminded Corey that what his wife was about to do was not small time. It wasn't a house in the hood. Nor was it a mom and pop shop fronting as a store for drug dealers. He and his wife were crossing over into what his father had wanted to do for so many years.

Corey and Mia kept their conversation limited as they entered the building. There wasn't much to say because they both were preoccupied in their own thoughts of the future.

"Welcome to the towers." A petite ginger twinkled.

"We're here to see Andrew Walsh." Corey was straight to the point. There wasn't much time for pleasantries.

"Yes." The woman's voice turned more serious. "You may take the private elevator to the left to the twelfth floor."

Corey put his hand on the small of his wife's back and walked to the elevator.

"He has a private elevator," Mia whispered.

"Yea, I've always wanted one," Corey joked.

"Maybe, after this, I'll buy you one," Mia countered with a wink.

The elevator was a quick ride. Upon exiting, they both were taken aback by the grandiose appearance of Andrew's office. Two armed guards, one tall and the other short and stocky, in black suits greeted them. The tall one approached Corey and the other intently watched. The burly man patted Corey down and used a wand to detect any metal. The same was done to Mia.

"Open your shirt," the tall guy said to Mia.

"I don't think so." Corey stepped in front of Mia.

"Sir, we're not here to look at your wife's goods. Believe me, we see plenty of perky ones on willing participants," the short and stocky guy countered.

"Okay, but I'm not sure of why you're looking," Corey said.

"You know what it is. Checking for wires."

"Get Andrew out here. We aren't wearing any wires and my wife is not about to be violated because you think we are working with the police." Corey's voice became louder.

"Seems like your wife is okay with it." The tall man smiled and nodded his head toward Mia.

Corey blood began to boil as he watched Mia open her blouse and reveal that she wasn't wearing a wire. Although a bra covered her, it was hard to stomach that she had to be subjected to such treatment.

"No wire," Mia stated then turned to Corey. "Your turn."

Corey lifted his shirt. Then slammed it down within seconds. Now, he was angry. She had decided to take matters in her own hands, reminding him of her shenanigans when working with Adrian.

"Let's go." The tall man ushered the two into Andrew's office.

The room appeared dark and presidential, as well as the blond-haired man who sat behind the desk. Everything about Andrew was Cimmerian. His blue eyes pierced them as they entered.

"Hello, Mr. and Mrs. Phillips." Andrew stood.

"Hello," Mia responded, but Corey said nothing.

"Well, I've definitely heard a lot about you, Mia, and I must say that I'm excited about working with you."

"Okay," Mia said as she reached to shake Andrew's hand.

"Mr. Phillips." Andrew extended his hand.

Corey returned a weak shake.

"Please have a seat." Andrew gestured for them to sit.

"Thanks." Mia attempted to be cordial.

"How have you been enjoying California?" Andrew asked. His eyes traveled the coils of Mia's exotic hair and mapped the planes of her high cheekbones and soft neck.

"Let's get to the point," Corey stated. "She's here to do business against her will."

"No, not against her will, Corey. Let's not jump to such harsh conclusions. You will be compensated well. You're safe. I guarantee it," Andrew said.

"Okay, so what do you need me to do?" Mia interrupted.

"In thirty days, I have almost a quarter of a billion dollars coming in from a business deal that has finally paid off. I need this money undetected. My usual connects can't handle that kind of flow. I was told that you can." Andrew again admired Mia's physique.

"How do you know about me?" Mia asked not yet ready to agree that she could handle such a job.

"I heard that you believe in God, Mrs. Phillips. Am I right?" Andrew asked.

"What kind of question is that, man?" Corey was irritated at Andrew's unfiltered admiration of Mia.

"I'm a believer," Mia responded as she placed her hand on Corey.

"Your God has been described as all seeing and all knowing— omniscient," Andrew said.

"Yes," Mia responded.

"I'm omniscient." Andrew smiled.

"That's a strong description, man." Corey frowned.

"Really? I know that you and your wife were once childhood sweethearts and that at the age of eighteen, Corey, you left abruptly to work for your washed-up father. Your brother, Keith, was killed in the street life that made you...how do you say...hood rich. Your beautiful wife is carrying your second biological child. And...I hate to be the bearer of bad news, Mia, but your husband lost his job over a month ago and he has yet to tell you. Seems as if his employers weren't too happy about him lying on his resume. He couldn't list former drug dealer on his app." Andrew leaned back in his chair to watch the revelation unfold.

Mia turned to Corey. "Did you lose your job?"

Corey felt a dagger drive through his heart. Andrew just summed up their current situation in seconds and now he would have to explain his employment status to his wife.

"It's a long story." Corey swallowed,

"Answer me!" Mia's anger twisted her face.

"I was fired." Corey decided to come clean.

"And you thought it was okay to keep that from me? Better yet, you create this lie each day having me believe that you are working from home to provide more support for me and the kids? Unbelievable." Mia shook her head.

"I'm sorry, but this is not the time nor the place to be talking about my job. This is much bigger." Corey spread his arms.

"Not really. I'm sleeping with the enemy and now I'm working for the enemy," Mia said.

"The enemy? I'm your husband. See that's why I didn't want to tell you. You can't handle change well. Your past has proven that," Corey said.

"Excuse me? I know you're not bringing up that." Mia's voice shook as Corey took aim at her for leaving the church and her family a few years ago after she found her ex-husband, Edward, and sister in bed together.

"I lost my job, Mia, because people don't like uncertainty. It makes them uneasy. I'm a thirty plus year old man who has no background, no job history. What do you think they would say if I put down I had ten years of experience in running the street without a felony? I can crunch numbers better than any of those guys working there, but because I have no history….well you know the rest," Corey said.

"Are you done? Because all that you are telling me still doesn't have anything to do with why you couldn't trust me enough to tell me." Mia looked at her husband.

"Yeah, I think I am." Corey stood and walked toward the door.

"When you're finished, I'll be outside the door. Holler if you need me."

Corey walked out the room.

"I'm sorry about that." Andrew handed Mia a few tissues.

"I don't want to be rude, but I don't need your sympathy. I really want to get this done," Mia stated.

"Alright then. I need a plan for my money."

"You said you have roughly two hundred and fifty million dollars that needs to be cleaned. It will cost you close to ten million upfront to legitimize it."

"That's a lot of money to lose up front." Andrew raised his eyebrow.

"Yeah, but you want to keep the government off your trail and I have a way to make up some of the costs."

"I'm listening."

Mia pulled a manila folder from her large purse and put it on the desk. Pulling a few sheets of paper from the folder, she began to unveil her plan.

"Amazing. You've come prepared without evening knowing what I want."

"I've found a few luxury properties in Beverly Hills up for silent auction in a few days." She pointed to the three homes shown on the paper. Mia ignored his comment. She had no idea what he wanted, but she had an idea. The L.A. black market knew her as a money launderer when she briefly chose a life of crime after her ex-husband and sister's affair.

"Okay." Andrew simply responded.

"These foreclosed homes total nine and a half million. This is a low ball number. These properties are well worth a total of five hundred million, but apparently the owners couldn't keep up with the mortgage. So, I guess that's lucky for you," Mia said.

"Hmmm, lucky for us." Andrew winked.

"You are going to buy those properties. Your company has more than enough buying power," Mia said as she pulled Andrew's financials from the folder.

"Oh, I see you've done your homework." Andrew's eyebrows quirked.

"You claim to be omniscient. I can't, but I can say that I do my homework. I want this done as quickly as possible. I have a family."

"It's not so bad here, you know." Andrew smiled.

Ignoring his statement, Mia continued, "You're going to buy the homes as rental properties for your employees. Now, you and I both know that your employees won't be staying there, but you can provide housing to some of the less favorable, nonetheless rich business associates for ten to twenty grand a month. In ninety days, the people who owe you two hundred and fifty million can buy the homes from you for that price."

"But you said the homes were worth half a billion dollars."

"They are, but all you need is half of that number. If you want to get some of your ten million investment you put in the homes, have them buy the homes but put a stipulation in writing that you will rent the homes and keep the rental profits for the next few years. They should be grateful because now your business partners have real estate worth a lot of money. Both parties are in a win situation."

"You make it sound easy."

"I'll act as your broker. The auction is the day after tomorrow. We'll bid online. If we don't get them, I have a few more homes that we can look at."

"I'm curious, with other options, why did you choose these homes?" Andrew asked.

Mia sighed. "Because I like them. They seem a bit more welcoming."

"I can buy you a home just like that. All you have to do is stay and work for me."

"Um, I'm going to pass, but thanks for the offer," Mia said.

"How about you and I talk more over dinner? No funny business. I know you're married." Andrew touched Mia's hand.

Moving her hand away, Mia said, "I really need to talk to Corey. He's waiting for me."

"I beg to differ. He left a few minutes ago." Andrew turned his computer monitor toward Mia so that she could see her husband as he walked from the building.

"What? Why? What is he doing?" Mia instantly felt tears sting the back of her eyes.

"He needs to cool off. Let him get some air. Come with me. We'll get dinner and I'll take you back to beach house," Andrew offered.

"I don't think so." Mia stood to leave.

"This is not a choice, Mia," Andrew countered.

"Well, if that's the case, I want seafood, king crab." Mia knew running from the office would never work. She desperately wanted to talk with Corey, but if he wanted to be a jerk and leave her in the hands of a criminal, then she would just have to comply.

"I know the perfect spot, let's go." Andrew stood.

Mia led the way unbeknownst to Andrew's admiration of her curves.

Chapter Twelve

Do not lie to one another, seeing that you have put off the old self with its practices and have put on the new self, which is being renewed in knowledge after the image of its creator.
COLOSSIANS 3:9-10 ESV

TYLER looked at Melody picking at her stuffed lobster tail. They sat in a five-star restaurant with prices on the menu that cost more than a car note. The way she was eating, they could have settled for the drive thru menu at any fast food burger joint.

"Baby, you're picking at your food." Tyler eyed the wasted food.

"I'm not that hungry," Melody replied.

"Then why are we here, babe? I asked if you were ready to eat and you said yes an hour ago. Had I known you were going to only take a few bites of your food, I wouldn't have made reservations."

The look that she gave him said it all. She was in no mood for his observations of her appetite.

"Alright. Why don't you tell me what's on your mind?" Tyler asked.

Melody sighed. "Why are we really here?"

"Because at least one of us is hungry," Tyler responded, then took a bite of one of the colossal coconut shrimp on his plate.

"You know what I mean. Why are we in Los Angeles? I mean, I know why we are here, but I feel like there is an urgency on your part."

"I know who killed Peyton." Tyler looked at his wife.

"We all do, but there is no proof. Being here will only make things worse." Melody huffed.

"No, I have proof and I'm here to get it," Tyler said.

"You've said that before, too."

"No, I'm serious. I know someone who is willing to work with us. This person witnessed it." Tyler's eyes turned dark from hurt and anger.

"What?" Melody whispered.

"It's only a matter of time. Andrew is going to have to pay one way or another," Tyler said.

"Okay, but we have to do this legally. There is no outlaw avenue for us. We have to be on the straight and narrow."

"You sound like my father."

"No, I sound like a woman who wants to have a future with her husband. I didn't sign up to be a widow or prisoner's wife." Melody became worried.

"That's farfetched. I have to make it right by Peyton."

"How is that? I mean, there was nothing you could've done, Tyler."

"I could've been there for her," he said.

"How?"

"I was preoccupied."

Melody became quiet in thought. Her mood was hooded as she looked at her husband.

"You mean, you were chasing after me at the time," Melody countered.

"I was preoccupied," Tyler repeated.

Melody removed her hand from his. "I see where this is going."

"Baby, I love you. You're my wife for life. Nothing will change that. I'm just saying that I was busy falling in love even when I knew my sister had a problem with depression."

"I can't compete with a dead person." Melody took a deep breath.

"No, you can't, and I'm not asking you, too. I'm asking you to give me a little time to work this out." Tyler pulled Melody's hand in his.

"I have a daughter who needs me."

"No, we have a daughter that needs us. That is not far from my mind. My sister lost her life. Let me show a little courtesy in trying to avenge her."

"Vengeance is the Lord's," Melody replied.

"So, the bible says," Tyler said.

"The bible says…" Melody's voice trailed as her attention went elsewhere.

"What?" Tyler's curiosity was piqued.

"My sister… My sister is here… My sister is here with another man." Melody's mouth dropped.

"What?" Tyler turned around. Goosebumps popped on his arms.

"She's with Andrew!" Melody nearly fainted.

"What the…" Tyler almost cursed.

"I'm going over there. She lied to me." Melody stood but was jerked down by Tyler.

"No, I don't want to make a scene," Tyler harshly whispered.

"My sister is with a criminal and by the looks of it she's quite comfortable with him. She's smiling. Oh, my goodness, Tyler, what is this?" Melody bellowed.

"I thought she told you that she and Corey were going to Miami for a few weeks," Tyler said.

"That's what she told me a few days ago. She said that she and Corey were going on a mini vacation." Melody stared at the couple.

"We have to leave. I don't want them to see us," Tyler said.

"It's pretty busy. We're in a secluded part. It would take much effort for them to see us." Melody wanted to know what was going on with her sister. She needed more time.

"We can't risk it. I hope Mia isn't involved with this man. Or for that matter, I hope she doesn't know anything about the cause of Peyton's death," Tyler murmured.

"My sister has nothing to do with your sister's death. I can guarantee that." Melody instantly became angry with the implication.

"I hope not." Tyler dismissed Melody's attitude and waved the waitress toward their table.

Tyler requested that the lady wrap their food up and bring it to the front of the restaurant. He left more than enough money on the table to take care of the meal, grabbed Melody by the hand, and nearly ran to the front of the place.

Tyler sat on the balcony of their hotel room and watched the night life below. He wasn't paying attention. His thoughts were on Mia. Why was she with Andrew? Did she know anything about the murder? If she did, then he would want her prosecuted, too. Then that meant Melody would have to choose between her husband and sister. Was that a risk he was willing to take?

Looking at the mini bar, he was tempted to pop a bottle to calm his racing thoughts. The enemy sure knew how to sprout a weed through a crack in the foundation. He never was one to tip the bottle, but tonight would be a great exception. He wanted to erase the image of Mia laughing with Andrew. Each time he tried, he saw the two of them cozy like a young giddy couple.

"I want to call my sister." Melody entered the terrace.

"You don't need my permission," Tyler responded.

"You're right. I don't, but as my husband, I'm letting you know," Melody said.

Tyler shrugged. "Do what makes you feel better. Whatever the case, I'm not stopping until I get answers."

"You've made that clear." Melody peered at Tyler.

"What are you waiting on? Your phone is in your purse. Do you want me to get it?"

"Do what makes you feel better," Melody countered.

"Reverse psychology doesn't work on me," Tyler said.

"Will a slap work?"

"Stop, Melody." Tyler walked past her and into the sitting room. He reached in her purse, pulled out the phone, and handed it to her.

Snatching it from him, she called Mia and placed the call on speaker.

"Hello?" Mia answered.

"Hey, sis," Melody responded.

"What's up buttercup? You miss me already?"

"How's Miami?" Melody asked.

"Beautiful. Corey and I have a beachfront. Can't complain a bit," Mia lied.

"Wow. So, are you two planning anything fun?" Melody asked.

"Yes, but we have really enjoyed just staying in."

"Tyler and I have decided to copy off you two," Melody said.

"Oh really? How copycat?"

"Tyler and I are visiting Los Angeles," Melody said.

"Really? I thought you wanted to stay clear of Los Angeles."

"Yeah, well, we are. We're in Beverly Hills. Just trying to relax and reevaluate a bit." Melody couldn't believe her sister could lie so easily. Mia sounded so convincing that for a brief moment Melody thought perhaps her sister had a doppelganger in Los Angeles.

"Okay." Mia's voice suddenly lost its tenacity.

"Maybe we can get together when you get back. You can come up here or I—" Melody was interrupted.

"Look, Melody, I have to go. Getting together sounds great. I'll call you." Mia didn't wait for her sister to say goodbye. She hung up.

Melody dabbed the corner of her eyes. She knew the last bit of their conversation sparked a bit of worry in Mia. At this point, she didn't care. Her sister had outright lied to her. Mia didn't know what Andrew was capable of doing. She didn't even know his involvement in Peyton's death. Melody was sure of it, but to convince her husband of Mia's innocence would prove to be hard.

"So, your sister is not being so truthful." Tyler looked at Melody.

"We're not being all the way truthful either. I didn't come out and tell her that we were out here being unsung detectives." Melody frowned.

"Alright. But, I need to know how Mia knows Andrew," Tyler said.

"Okay and how are you going to go about doing that?"

"I've hired a private investigator," Tyler responded.

"Okay." Melody threw her hands in the hair.

"I'm going to bed. I have a long day tomorrow."

"So, you're leaving me out of this?" Melody asked.

"No. Get some rest. Go shopping. Enjoy the day. We'll meet up around six o'clock and eat dinner in the restaurant downstairs."

"So sayeth the king." Melody walked back to the balcony and listened to the sleepless city below.

Chapter Thirteen

By insolence comes nothing but strife, but with those who take advice is wisdom. PROVERBS 13:10 ESV

THE sound of people, parties, and cars filled the night air as Corey walked the streets. The nostalgia of being close to the ocean and a step from making all your dreams come true was thick in the air. Corey took a deep breath.

He knew he had been wrong for leaving his wife in the presence of Andrew. He was aware of wrong the moment he stepped from the building because guilt sucker punched him. Yet, somehow, pride kept him from stopping and going back. His insolence caused him strife.

Mia apparently had everything under control. She popped her blouse wide open to show her lacy, black bra and she callously unleashed wrath about his employment situation. He should have told her, but again the ugly head of pride and guilt for not being able to take care of his family choked the truth from him.

It was well past ten and it was time for him to head back to the house. Lucky for him, the place wasn't that far. Quickening his pace, Corey maneuvered his way through the loud crowd.

"Hey, sexy!" A tall woman touched his arm.

Corey recognized Camila Hernandez. She was an old flame who ran the streets with him from time to time before he moved to

Indianapolis. "Hi, how are you?" Corey really had no time to catch up with her. Besides, he was happily married. Well, at least before the fiasco in Andrew's office.

"Been missing you, boo." Camila placed her hand on him and slung her long dark hair over her shoulder. The tresses fell slightly past her waist, reminding Corey of how he used to run his fingers through her hair.

"Yeah, well, I have a different life now." Corey smiled

"So, I heard. A little birdie told me that you left the streets for a church girl." Camila laughed.

"Yeah, something like that," Corey said.

"Hmm, so where is she now?" Camila looked around.

"Waiting on me," Corey said.

"Can you make her wait a little longer? I would love to…talk with you a bit more, Daddy. It's been so long. Don't you miss our late nights and early mornings?" Camila licked her lips and winked.

Corey wondered why some single women wanted to interject themselves into a marriage. Yes, he remembered the times they had together. They were amazing, but when it was over, it was over. When Camila left his bed, there was no desire to call her and invite her to dinner. There was no loneliness experienced when she was away. Weeks could go by before he saw her again. So, why hadn't he just walked away from the conversation they were having now?

"Yeah, I remember," Corey said.

"So, what's it going to be, baby? I got a place just up the street." Camila stepped closer and Corey could smell the liquor, and it burned his nostrils. The scent was familiar because they both used to get tipsy off the same gin.

"Naw, Cami, I gotta go. I'm a married man now. It was good seeing you." He smiled.

"Good seeing you, too. I'm jealous. A guy like you falling in love. Hmmm great catch. Lucky girl." Cami gave a friendly pout by pursing her lips.

"Take care." Corey started to turn away, but her hand touched him once more.

Corey watched as Camila wrote on the back of a business card.

"Take this. If the wife thing doesn't work out, give me a call." Camila pushed the paper into his pants pocket.

Corey had no intention to use it but didn't want to offend her or cause an unwanted scene.

"See you around." Corey walked away.

He'd spent enough time walking around in his thoughts. It was time to get back to Mia. He didn't want to be the source of her stress. She was carrying his baby, and he should be home rubbing her feet. Having another child now wasn't in the plan, but if he was going to bring life into the world, he wanted it to be through her.

Deciding to cut through a much quieter street, Corey would be able to get home faster. He didn't want to run into anymore old friends. Camila was enough. The dark street only had a few people. Just the way he needed it to be, or so he thought.

Corey was in tune with the hood and the black utility van with tented windows seemed out of place parked along the street with the luxury cars. Especially, the burly man who was standing on the driver side of the van smoking a cigarette. The darkness concealed his face.

Uneasiness settled within him. Fear didn't come easy to him, but danger was imminent. Turning back now would appear cowardice.

"Stop being a punk, man. Indy has made you soft," Corey whispered to himself as he continued walking toward the van.

Corey's hand touched the back of his jeans. These were the moments he wished he had his gun tucked in the waistband of his pants.

Red embers bounced off the sidewalk as the man flicked his cigarette to the ground. An adrenaline rush overcame him as he watched another hooded man exit the vehicle. They both nodded at one another and for a brief moment Corey felt silly for anticipating an altercation.

"This is crazy." Corey rubbed his hand over his face. "I'm getting too old for—"

The loud noise of the sliding van door echoed in the quiet. Feet shuffled, and before Corey could fully turn around, a blackness covered his face. It took him a moment to realize a hood had been placed over his head.

"What the hell are you doing?" Corey screamed. The air was thick in the mask and his attempt to wrestle it off did nothing to ease the heat he felt surrounding his head. His heart jackhammered in his chest.

"Shut up and get in," a voice demanded.

"No," Corey responded.

"Don't resist. It will only make it harder."

"I got a family. I'm not going willingly." Corey tried to jerk away again.

"Man, show this fighter how to let go," the same voice commanded.

Corey's eyes bugged. He tried to see through the mask, put his attempt was futile. Within moments, he felt a tight restraint around his neck. His arms were pinned behind him and his eyes felt as if they were about to pop out of his head. Pressure built in his head and streaks of light flashed through his vision. Numbness made him feel dizzy and more darkness overcame him. His last thoughts were of his wife waiting for him at the beach house. In moments, his lifeless body was pushed into the cold floor of the van. No one even noticed as the vehicle screeched off into the night.

Mia sat on the couch in the living room. Hours had passed since she came home from her dinner with Andrew. Now her annoyance had changed into worry. She'd texted Corey several times with no answer. That wasn't like him. Even when they were upset with one another, they wouldn't stop communicating through texts. Earlier, her frustration with her husband's lie, she'd been abrupt and now she regretted her actions. They're thousands of miles away from home doing something completely illegal. There was no time for division.

Who could she call to let them know her man wasn't at home in the wee hours of the morning? The truth would be out then and once again her family would be in complete panic mode reliving her escapade to Los Angeles after she caught Melody with Edward.

Melody. Her sister called when Andrew's driving service was taking her home. Everything was fine as it could be until Melody mentioned that she and Tyler were in L.A. Why on Earth would they come here after Peyton was murdered here? Melody didn't mention the Deen family's affairs much, but when she did, it was always about Tyler's dogmatic search for finding the person responsible for the death of his sister. Mia sometimes wished Tyler would find the killer so her sister could live a normal life. The last three years had been rocky for her. It had been for all of them.

Mia's racing thoughts shifted to Edward. Taking a deep breath, she thought of her ex-husband. She hadn't seen him in months and was grateful. He was in bad shape. Alcohol was his best friend and grief was a first cousin. A few months ago, she wanted to see if he was capable of spending time with Taylor. He wasn't. His efficiency apartment was in shambles and he kept a revolving door to prostitutes willing to deal with his rude behavior. Perhaps, if Edward had never cheated, then she wouldn't be here working for Andrew. That was a tough pill to swallow, because had Edward not have committed adultery then she would have never married Corey. Corey was her man, her best friend, her lover, her provider, and her chivalrous knight.

The clock now read 2:00 a.m. and there was still no Corey. Picking up the phone, Mia called him again. This time, it went to voicemail. She screamed with frustration and slammed her mobile device on the couch.

"God, please," Mia screamed.

Helplessness took residence in the pit of her stomach. How could she call on God now? Everything she was doing was out of fear. Some way she lost her trust in God and delivered herself into the hands of the enemy once again.

The phone buzzed and Mia jerked to reach for it. A single message was displayed on the screen from Corey.

I'm cool. Don't worry.

Chapter Fourteen

Even though I walk through the valley of the shadow of death... PSALM 23:4 ESV

TYLER arrived. His GPS had given him quite the challenge, but finally he showed up at his destination. A nearly empty parking lot lay between two large buildings. Putting his hand to his brow, Tyler looked up to the sky. The two colossal buildings that he stood between reminded him of steep mountains. He was below, stuck in a valley. Their large presence cast shadows on the ground making the lot appear dark and gloomy. The few abandoned cars were sporadically parked, giving an eerie feeling of danger and isolation, perhaps even death.

The contact wanted to meet off the grid and this was definitely the spot. This was also a place that if something were to happen to him, no one would know where to look. Small hairs stood at attention on his arms in anticipation, but determination kept his feet glued to the pavement.

A loud whistle penetrated the silence and he turned his head in the sound of the direction. He was able to make out a silhouette of a person in dark attire standing by the entrance of the garage. Uncertainty flooded him, but there was no turning back. He was about to receive the answers that he waited for such a long time. His longsuffering was due payment.

Leaving his rental, Tyler headed toward the door. Once hooded features became clear, revealing a tall, brunette woman. Her tight bun at the nape of her neck, chiseled features, and tight lips meant no nonsense. Tyler nodded and attempted to shake her hand, but she was more concerned if whether or not he was being followed. Her eyes wildly shifted around the lot.

"Hi, I'm—" Tyler was cut off.

"I know who you are, Mr. Deen. Let's save those introductions for inside. Thanks." She gestured for him to enter.

"Thank you," Tyler responded as he walked through.

Stepping in front of him, she quickly walked down the stairs. "Follow me."

Tyler nodded and tried to keep up. Wide eyed, he took in the spacious places. From the outside, the parking garage appeared as just that, a place where cars parked. Now, he realized this was much more. This was a front that resembled a secluded warehouse.

The large open space was endless and reminded Tyler of a covert government agency. People were working on computers, looking at large monitors mounted on the wall, and reviewing pictures of high profile criminals.

"Here." The woman pointed to a small table that sat two other people. They were just as serious as the woman. Eyes scanned him and offered no smile.

"Tyler," the woman began as she sat down, "my name is Melanie Stevens. I'm an agent for a special branch of the FBI. We focus on illegal drugs and human trafficking."

Tyler was grateful that his connect was no criminal, but someone he could possibly trust. At least he hoped, because he was smart enough to know that even dirty people held badges. "Nice to meet you."

"I guess I can say the same, but under different circumstances… I knew your sister and before she died, she was making an attempt to turn in evidence that would permanently shut down Andrew's operations."

"You mean my sister was trying to get out?" Tyler said.

"Yes, she was. We were planning to put her in witness protection once she retrieved the information, but that never happened."

"What?" Tyler shook his head.

"Yes, Andrew proves to be a powerful man."

"So, you put my baby sister in danger?" Tyler asked.

'No, Mr. Deen, your sister put herself in danger the moment she became his mistress." Melanie pushed a few pictures of Peyton sitting on Andrew's lap, proving her statement.

"Maybe. So, how are you going to get more evidence? I want this man behind bars," Tyler raged.

"We have reason to believe that your sister-in-law is working for him. We need to get to her," Melanie said.

"I knew something wasn't right when I saw her the other day with Andrew."

"Yeah, well, we also have reason to believe that Andrew is making her do this against her will."

"What? What do you mean?" Tyler asked

Melanie nodded her head to one of the gentlemen at the table. The red headed guy got up from the table and headed toward a small dry-walled room that oddly sat in the wide-open space of the warehouse. It was the only part of the building that was closed off to everyone. The man returned with a tired and bruised Corey.

"What is this?" Tyler jumped from his seat. "Man, are you alright?"

"Yeah, bro." Corey's eyes were red.

Tyler gave him a quick hug and remained standing.

"Mr. Phillips has given us the truth and we want to help. We think Mr. and Mrs. Phillips can set a trap for Andrew."

"You mean you can get them killed like my sister. Please!" Tyler huffed.

"And there'll be no guarantees that when Andrew gets caught, that your in-laws won't be free from prosecution. It's best to work with us." Melanie shrugged.

"This is crazy. You're basically blackmailing my family to work for you." Andrew eyes bugged with anger.

"No, your sister-in-law, Mia, has a very interesting background that I'm sure would be great table talk over steak and a bottle of wine." Melanie's sarcasm did not go unnoticed.

"We don't drink," Tyler retaliated.

"Too bad because once you hear her story, you're going to want to knock a few back."

"Yes, I feel like a cold one right, now," Corey muttered.

"Are you serious right now?" Tyler looked at Corey and shook his head.

"Man, I need something," Corey responded.

"I got one in the back." Melanie finally smiled.

"No, we won't be drinking. Look, I don't know what you have on Mia, but what you are asking my family to do is risky. I mean, lives are at stake."

"It is what it is," Melanie responded.

"I can't believe this." Tyler shook his head.

"I'll tell you what, I'll give you a few days to give me a decision. I'll contact you. I am sure that once you think it all over, you'll realize that working with us is the better option."

"Yeah," Tyler began then turned toward Corey. "Let's go, bro."

Corey said nothing as he started walking toward the exit.

"Good day, gentlemen." Melanie smiled.

Tyler nodded and followed his brother-in-law. He had a million questions about Mia that needed to be answered.

Mia's nerves were shattered as she sat in Andrew's office looking over documents. Her sister was in Los Angeles and Corey didn't come home last night. Mia was convinced that his night out was her fault. She was sure that when she woke up, her man would be at least on the coach, but when morning came, disappointment set in because her husband was not there. Calling him over and over proved to bring no results. Her calls went straight to his voicemail. Her thoughts went straight to negativity.

Regret traveled through her and she felt wedged in the valley between anguish and fury. Perhaps she had been too hard on him, but it was too late now. The verbal daggers had been thrown and now she sat once again in the throne of sin.

"Hi, beautiful." Andrew smiled as he walked into the large conference room.

"Hello." Mia was not thrilled with the idea of responding to his subtle flirting, but right now she needed to keep the peace if she wanted out.

"So, you agree?" Andrew stood behind her.

"With what?" Mia was uncomfortable with his nearness.

"That you're beautiful." Andrew touched Mia's hair, and then sat down in the adjacent chair.

"Um, I am not sure how to answer that." Mia glanced at him then back at the screen.

"I wish you did. So, did you and the hubby reconcile?" Andrew smiled.

"I..." Mia was about to mention that she had not seen her husband but decided against it. The less that Andrew knew of her marital issues, the better. "We're fine."

"Good for him." Andrew nodded. "So, we are ready to move forward?"

"Yes. Documents look good." Mia attempted to smile.

"Share," Andrew said.

"Share what?" Mia's eyebrows quirked.

"Your thoughts, Mia." Andrew ogled her.

Mia realized there was no point in lying. "I want to know will this be it. I don't want to live in fear thinking that I'll have to do this again six months from now, a year from now, five years from now."

"Why are you worried? I've given you nothing but the best. I've not hurt you. You came here looking for a way out of a financial bind. You and your husband needed it," Andrew said.

Mia shook her head. "No, I came here because Tennessee threatened my family. I won't deny truth in that we might need some money, but not this money."

Andrew was silent for a moment. Lines of thought appeared on his forehead. His face was unreadable, but his countenance whispered confusion.

"So, you are here out of fear, because our mutual acquaintance threatened your family?"

"Yes. You didn't know? I'm not here because of the almighty dollar, Andrew. I'm here for the preservation of my family."

Silence enveloped them once again before Andrew stood and walked toward Mia. Unsure of his actions, Mia stood as well. Her breathing quickened as he intently watched her. Warm hands slid around her neck and Mia watched the pupils of Andrew's icy blue eyes constrict into pin points. Their close proximity bothered her as she could feel his fingers tremble.

"Are you afraid of me?" Andrew asked.

"Do I need to be?" Mia shot back.

Andrew's top lip quivered. "I'm a man trying to make money. That's all. You have nothing to fear unless you cross me."

"I'm a woman who wants to protect her family and you have nothing to fear unless you hurt them." Mia gently removed Andrew's hands from her neck and took a step back. "Now, I need to know that once I do this for you, there'll be no more contact."

Andrew stepped forward once again closing the space between them. "Maybe, I don't want you to go. But, I don't take too kindly in Tennessee threatening one of my employees. It took a great deal for me to get to you. A man like me can't let a prize slip through his fingers."

"I won't work for you. I've got to go home. I have a husband, a family... A church." Mia's voice began to shake.

"Church girl?" Andrew's eyes sparked. "I knew a church girl once. She left God for me. We had a good time."

"Well, I'm sorry to disappoint you, but I won't be the one to provide a good time." Mia stepped away, but this time she grabbed her purse to exit the room.

"What? No dinner?" Andrew laughed as he watched her walk away. Her hips called him and he once again wondered how it would feel to have a woman like that by his side.

Chapter Fifteen

Beloved, never avenge yourselves, but leave it to the wrath of God, for it is written, "Vengeance is mine, I will repay, says the Lord." ROMANS 12:19 ESV

MELODY watched the clock. Tyler was taking an exceptionally long time to get home. This trip had proven to be more stressful than she had originally thought. She knew he would be poking a sleeping bear, but she didn't imagine that he would all out kick the beast in the butt with cleats. Now that her sister was somehow waltzing with the enemy, Tyler was ready to burst.

Instead of worrying, Melody picked up the phone to get answers. She called Mia.

"Hello?" Mia answered after the first ring.

"Wow, you must have been waiting on my phone call." Melody attempted to laugh.

"What's up, sis? I'm kind of busy," Mia clipped.

"Oh, so it's like that now?" Melody pushed.

"Melody, what do you want? I really don't have time for this." Mia sighed.

"Okay, so I should just cut to the chase," Melody's pushed.

"Pretty much, sis," Mia said.

"Why are you lying to me?" Melody asked.

"I'm not sure what you mean. Lying to you? Really?" Mia shot back.

"Oh, so you aren't lying to me?"

"No!"

"Then tell me why you're in Los Angeles hanging out with the man who killed Peyton? Tell me that, sis, because Tyler is ready to send you to jail and me to divorce court for supporting your craziness. For now, I'm on your side."

"You're on my side?" Mia's voice rose.

"Yeah, I am," Melody responded.

"Then if you're on my side, back the hell up. Messing around with Andrew will put you in the grave. Right now, I'm a dead woman walking. Get Tyler and get out of L.A. Do you hear me? Get out of L.A., Melody, and don't come back. You know you and Tyler are responsible for Taylor and CJ if something happens to me. Get my kids. Make sure they're okay. Do you hear me?" Mia cried.

"Let me help you." Melody's throat was tight with pain.

"Get out of L.A. Get my kids. Promise me."

"I promise, sis," Melody cried, too.

Mia ended the call first.

"What are you promising?"

Melody turned to see her husband looming by the door. The tired look on his face meant he didn't have time for her to beat around the bush.

"That if something happens to my sister, then I would take her kids and I would…" Melody hesitated.

"What?" Tyler walked closer. "You would what?"

"I would get on a plane as soon as I can to ensure the safety of her children… And my child." Melody swallowed.

"So, this tells me two things." Tyler's eyes pierced her. "You know your sister is conspiring with the enemy who killed my sister and that you're willing to do anything to protect your own even when you know she is guilty."

"Let me tell you something, Tyler, your sister decided to dance with the enemy way before mine even thought about Andrew. As a matter of fact, perhaps, and I'm speculating, I'm thinking, had it not been for Peyton coming to California, then somehow Mia wouldn't even be in this mess."

"That's farfetched, Melody and you know it."

"And so are your actions in this suicide mission to avenge your sister. We could be busy making babies, but you want to bury a man."

"He killed my sister." Tyler's voice cracked.

"Yes, he did, and it is not for you to determine his fate, or have you forgotten the Word of God?" Melody shot back.

"Don't bring God into this."

"Listen to these words, dearly beloved, avenge not yourselves, but rather give place unto wrath, for it is written, vengeance *is* mine, I will repay, saith the Lord."

"Really? You know what? Maybe, if I wasn't chasing you around, I would have been able to save my sister." Tyler kicked a table.

More tears came quickly. Words almost escaped Melody as she looked at her husband. "I'm going to act like I didn't hear you say that. You get one lifetime pass for reckless words and you just used yours. I can't take the blame for Peyton. I won't be the scapegoat for your parents' fault and Peyton's psychosis. I'm packing my things. I'm going to ensure that out of the Deen and Phillips family, there is a survivor to take care of the three children who have been left home while their parents are out her playing cops and robbers."

"So, you're leaving?"

"Yeah, I am. And you know what? Don't have me there waiting too long. I want a family. I want a chance to love a man who loves God. God gave me you. Don't mess it up."

"Are you threatening to leave me?"

"I'm saying that you need to make a choice and I can't do that for you. I'm in the land of the living. I'm taking care of the one's that are alive because at the end of the day, you trying to kill Andrew, locking him up, beating him senseless won't bring your dead sister back."

"Yeah, it's best you go home." Tyler could hardly contain his anger.

"You're right. I can't compete with a dead woman." Melody walked to the closet and grabbed her coat.

"Where are you going? It's too late to be out." Tyler grabbed for Melody's arm.

"Don't worry about me. Worry about your sister. Something might happen to her." Melody snatched away and walked toward the door.

"Don't you want to know what happened at my meeting? I saw Corey. I talked with the FBI. Something might be worked out if Mia can set Andrew up." Tyler tried to prolong the conversation.

"I don't care. Who cares? It doesn't matter anyway. Seems to me that if the FBI is looking for Andrew, then we are in a much bigger mess. I'm gone," Melody said.

"You forgot your things. Don't you have to pack?" Tyler called after

"Ship them." Melody continued to walk.

Corey watched Mia as she worked on her laptop. She didn't know that he had finally returned as he watched from outside. She sat on the couch with her head in her hands. Her delicate fingers massaged her temple. He knew she was stressed and even in her current state, was beautiful. Somehow, he'd managed to get an opportunity to marry her. God blessed him and now he wondered if his gift was only for a season. If he never would have brought her to California after her ex-husband had cheated, she wouldn't be in this mess. Better yet, if he'd only stayed in Indy when Adrian came nearly thirteen years ago, he would have been Mia's first husband and all this mess would never have come to pass.

They would never be free and believing they would made them fools. They had played house for a little over two years, but the streets now wanted what it had once loosed.

Opening the door, Corey braced himself for Mia's wrath. He'd been gone for over 24 hours.

"Hi, baby." He placed his arms around her.

"Hi, baby," Mia responded and continued with her work.

He wasn't sure of how to accept her calm, but he would go with it.

"About last night—" Corey began.

"Let's not worry about that." Mia kept typing. Her nails noisily hit the keyboard and Corey wondered if the computer would break at her pounding. Yeah, she was mad.

"I just want you to know that—" Corey was interrupted.

"I thought I told you that it's really nothing to discuss."

"Really?" Corey asked.

"I mean, is it really? You left your pregnant wife with a criminal and then didn't come home last night. I guess if you're comfortable with that, then what possibly is there to talk about? There couldn't be any excuse that you could give that could justify your recklessness." Mia stopped typing and was now peering at him.

"Yes, I have a good excuse. A real good one," Corey said, pulling Mia to her feet. She didn't resist, but her eyes shot daggers as he took her outside on the porch. He closed the door behind them.

"Is it necessary for us to be outside?" Mia huffed and then folded her arms across her chest as the cool air grazed her arms.

"Yes, this house could be bugged and what I'm about to tell you is only for your ears." Corey pulled his hoody off and put it on Mia.

"Do tell." Mia rolled her eyes.

"I was kidnapped."

Silence rested in the air as Mia studied Corey. She was unreadable. He knew that his response was hard to believe, but it was the truth nonetheless.

"Okay and they just let you go?" Mia rolled her eyes.

"Look, I was snatched off the streets by some special government agency that deals with trafficking. You wouldn't believe this, but Tyler was there."

Mia sighed. "Okay, I'm listening."

"They want us to set up Andrew. They believe he killed Peyton, but they need to get him on much more than him killing Peyton," Corey said.

"And we're just going to go set him up and live to tell about it?" Mia threw up her arms in exasperation.

"Yes, pretty much. We don't have a choice." Corey held Mia's hand to pull her close.

"Why not? We can refuse," Mia said.

"We can, but if we do, then we are going to be charged with a federal crime. Money laundering. Thirty-five years."

"What?" Mia nearly shrieked. "Corey, what is this?"

"We don't have a choice, baby. We set him up, we get out of this. We don't, then we don't see our kids. Our marriage, us… I can't let that happen."

"Look, baby. We can send for the kids. We can run. Leave the country. Start over," Mia said.

"With what money, baby?" Corey knew they probably would only last a year on Mia's savings.

"Look, I have access to Andrew's accounts. I can set up an offshore account and wire any amount we desire into it. It would be untraceable. We'd be set for life. We can go live in some other country. Somewhere. He'll never find us. He'll never touch our kids," Mia cried.

Instantly, Corey's heart shattered into pieces. Helplessness gripped him and he wondered where God was in this very instant because right now he felt abandoned by the one that had given His word that He would protect them.

"No, we can't do that. Andrew would look for us until the day he dies. But I have a solution." Corey's voice shook.

"What?" Mia now had her arms wrapped around her husband with her head resting on his chest.

"Trust me."

"Okay."

Corey held his wife close. Her pain and worry consumed him. It was clear. He would call Adrian. He was back in the game. They would go underground, but under the protection of the Phillips' cartel. No one would hurt his family and they wouldn't have to hide because they had taken another man's spoils. Selling was not something he wanted to do, but watching his wife suffer was worse than stepping back into the streets that had claimed Keith and Swift. He once had the law on his bankroll, too. Once they knew he was back, it wouldn't take long to get them back on the books.

God had given him no choice. This time, he couldn't wait on God. Waiting would cause his family to die and that, he wasn't willing to sacrifice.

Chapter Sixteen

You have heard that it was said to those of old, 'You shall not murder; and whoever murders will be liable to judgment.
MATTHEW 5:21 ESV

IT was late night and Melody was relieved to finally be home. She wasn't yet sure of the excuse she would give for returning without her husband, but at this point she didn't care. She needed to see her daughter, Lena.

The family estate was lit up like a Christmas tree on their cul de sac. The glow from the outside lightening was the Deen residential trademark. It was ironic that their luminous home gave off such light, but the present situation screamed darkness. Sighing, Melody tried to remain positive and think about Lena. As much as she wanted to hold her bundle of joy, it was well past the little girl's bed time. Perhaps it was good to see her in the morning. By then, Melody would have come up with a believable story about Tyler's absence. The truth would certainly put the household into an uproar.

She put her key in the door and was met with the unexpected.

"What are you doing here?" Charles sat in the darkness.

"What are you doing here?" Melody returned the question as she turned on the light.

Charles sat on their settee with papers surrounding him. A small flashlight was in his hand.

"I'm trying to figure out why you and Tyler are in Los Angeles," Charles said.

Anger struck her as she realized Charles had been going through Tyler's personal papers.

"You are pushing the line. You have no business digging through our things, let alone breaking and entering."

"Breaking and entering? This is my property. I pay the mortgage." Charles sneered. "Now answer my question. What are you doing here?"

"Well, I decided to come home. I put the key in the lock. I was about to go take a shower. Then I was going to lay down. That's what I'm doing here." Melody pointed to the ground then slung her purse on the chair. She knew she would irritate him with sarcasm.

"Don't play games with me, dear."

"Oh, you started game playing the moment that you hid evidence that pinned Peyton's death to Andrew. You rolled the dice when you broke into my house and riffled through my things, Charles. I'm telling Tyler about this."

"I don't care. Where is my son?" Charles asked.

"He's still in Los Angeles." Melody decided to tell the truth.

"Doing what?"

"What do you think? I mean, what has he been doing for the past eighteen months. He's been a pastor, a husband, a detective, and now a vigilante."

"He shouldn't be doing this." Charles stood.

"No, he shouldn't, but at this point, his heart is broken wondering how he can avenge his sister. Honestly, I'm not sure what he will try to do to Andrew." Melody sighed.

"And you left him there?" Charles accusatory tone did not sit well with Melody.

"Yes."

"Wow, some wife," Charles shot back.

"Some father you are. Tyler is trying to do what you couldn't and wouldn't do. And I'm trying to stay alive for my daughter and my..." Melody stopped. There was no need to bring Mia's name into this. Charles knew nothing of her past and it was better for it to stay that way.

"I'm sorry, Melody. I... I wish I could have been a better father to Peyton. I miss her and God knows Amelia does, too."

"I know, but look, at some point we are going to have to let go because Peyton's death is equivalent to us walking in death. I want to live, Charles." Melody pointed to herself. "My husband is running around Los Angeles and at the rate he is going, I don't think he's going to come back alive." Tears streamed her face.

Charles walked over to Melody and placed his arms around her. Her head rested on his chest and she wept.

"Don't worry, daughter. Tyler is a smart man. He will come to his senses. He has always been stubborn, but he loves you. His love for you surpasses his desire for revenge," Charles whispered.

"I just want him home," Melody said.

"I know, dear."

"I won't bring this up to Amelia."

Melody stepped back. "Yes, that is a good idea. She is not ready for any more bad news."

"I know. She has definitely turned around for the better since Brandy has been here. In just a few short days, I can see my old wife peeking through."

"Yes, as far as she is concerned, I came back early because Tyler has to take care of unexpected business and I missed Lena."

"Sounds like a plan."

"How are you going to avoid Amelia's questions about Tyler?" Melody asked.

"No worries. No worries." Charles smiled through tired eyes.

"Okay."

"Get some rest. Let us watch our granddaughter for one more night and then you can come get her when you're rested." Charles patted Melody's arm.

"Okay."

Charles chuckled. "I haven't heard these many okays since, well since never."

"Let's just say, right now, we're fighting on the same team." Melody smiled.

"What?" Charles exaggerated, "Team Deen."

"Yeah," Melody said.

"So, you'll be okay tonight?" Charles started to leave.

"Yes, I mean, Tyler and I didn't leave on good terms, but I...I don't know."

"You made a choice to live. Sometimes you have to be the first to make a move. He'll be back." Charles nodded and then left the guest house.

"I hope so," Melody whispered.

Edward paced the small room like a caged tiger. He'd been in this place for days and needed to get out. The residents in the facility were certifiably crazy and it had been an insult to think his doctor thought of him nuts, too. Edward only needed his wife back and if he could just rewind time, everything would be okay.

"Hello, Edward. You're up early." Deon, one of the medical assistants, entered the room.

"Yeah," Edward mumbled as he watched the large man drop pills into a cup. He knew the routine. Blue pill for moods. White pills for anxiety. And a tan pill for peace. Edward wondered for whose peace, his or society's? There would be none today because he would be leaving soon.

"How many more days?" Edward asked Deon.

"You're not happy here?" Deon smiled, but continued to work. Edward sneered at the man's condescending remark. Of course he wasn't happy in this hell hole.

"I guess. I thought I'd be here for a few days, but the doc says more. Feeling a little stir crazy if you know what I mean." Edward approached Deon which caused the medical assistant to stop.

"Okay. I'm thinking that I might have misread your charts. Doc must have increased your milligrams on the blue pills." Deon scanned Edward then glanced at the chart attached to the bed.

Rage crept within Edward. Deon was a handsome young man that had a life in front of him. Why couldn't he have a life as such?

"You married?" Edward noticed a simple gold band on Deon's finger.

"Yeah." Deon's expression became serious. "You need to rest." Deon attempted to guide Edward to the sofa.

"Get off me!" Edward snatched away. "So, you have a wife. I do, too. I need to get to her."

"Calm down. You know the truth. Remember the truth. You are no longer married." Deon watched Edward.

"Are you a faithful man?" Envy pulsed through Edward.

"This isn't about me." Deon shook his head.

"Answer me!"

Deon started for the door but was not quick enough. Edward put his arm around Deon's neck and squeezed. A desperate yelp escaped Deon, but the crushing force on his windpipe only allowed his call for help to be a whispery plea.

Edward only wanted to put the man to sleep, but Deon struggled with flaying arms and kicking feet and that enrage Edward. What was meant to be a temporary hold became much more. Deon's legs buckled and his limbs gave sporadic jerky movements as Edward squeezed harder. Beads of perspiration tapered Edward's brow as he felt the pinned stress and of hurt of Mia's betrayal leave him by clutching Deon's neck.

"It's better this way. Your wife will leave you as soon as you mess up. They always do," Edward whispered. Deon blinked wildly, and then suddenly the man became limp.

Keeping his arm around Deon's neck, Edward loosened his grip and watched the door. He waited to make sure no one entered. After glancing at the shiny wedding band on Deon's finger, Edward pulled it off. The simple white gold band resembled the one that he had shared with Mia. He slipped it on, stood, and locked the door. It was time to go. He dragged the lifeless body of Deon into the restroom and quickly changed his clothing. Someone would be looking for Deon soon, if not already. He needed to get to Mia. He needed for her to hear him out be any means necessary. Taking Deon's life hadn't been hard. It was rather gratifying for someone to feel the same helpless that he had felt. If he had to take Corey's then so be it, but someone was going to hear him. He needed that someone to be Mia.

Using Deon's keycard to exit the patients' floor had been relatively easy. No one seemed to pay attention to him at all. Edward figured that most people wouldn't expect to have a patient to escape the facility. That's what was wrong with people. They were gullible.

Edward pulled Deon's phone from his pocket and dialed his daughter's number.

"Hello?" Taylor answered.

"Hey, baby girl," Edward said as he took Deon's wallet.

"Dad! How are you? I've been trying to reach you. Your phone has been going straight to voicemail. Whose number is this?" Taylor was talking a mile a minute.

"A friends. I miss you." Edward didn't give information about his extended absence.

"Wow. Well, at least you called," Taylor said.

"Your mom home yet?" Edward asked.

"No, Pop and Mom are still in Los Angeles. They should be home in a week or so," Taylor said.

"Alright, well, I'm thinking I might be able to come see you soon. If that is alright with you." Edward heard sirens in the distance and wondered if Deon's body had been found. He needed to get out of plain sight.

"Um, okay, I'm sure you'll have to talk with Mom about that." Taylor was a bit skeptical.

"Yeah, well sweetheart, Daddy has to go. I'll get a back to you soon. I love you." Edward saw the police cars pull up in front of the building from across the street.

"Okay, love you, too," Taylor responded.

Edward disconnected the call, pulled the baseball cap tighter on his head and blended with the afternoon crowd in the park.

He needed to get money for a plane ticket. His plan was to buy a ticket with Deon's credit card, but that was easily traceable. He would buy a prepaid card and execute his alternative plan.

Chapter Seventeen

Brothers, I do not consider that I have made it my own. But one thing I do: forgetting what lies behind and straining forward to what lies ahead. Philippians 3:13 ESV

MELODY'S eyes popped open around noon. Turning her body, she groaned. Her arms and legs were bricks. She wasn't surprised at her sluggishness. A week in L.A. and she'd become jet lagged. A sudden wave of nausea paused her steps as she got out of bed. Queasiness had greeted her a few times while in L.A. and she hoped she wasn't getting sick. A virus was far from what she needed right now. There was too much to do.

She and Lena would soon be hopping in the car to care for her niece and nephew. She'd made Mia a promise and she wasn't planning on breaking it because of a silly little illness. Plus, she needed a distraction to her painful thoughts of Tyler.

Melody attempted to move one more time from the bed. Peeking in Lena's room, she was grateful. Her baby was still sleep. They stayed up late and Lena was a sure thing when sleeping eight to 10 hours straight.

Her phone rang.

"Hello?" Melody saw her husband's photo displayed on her phone. She hadn't talked to him since she walked out of their hotel room two days ago. They had only sent short texts, but nothing more.

"Baby?" Tyler's voice came across tired and weak.

"Hi," Melody said.

"I miss you. I love you, baby."

"I love you, too."

"I don't want you to be mad at me," Tyler nearly whispered.

"I'm not. I just want you to come home."

Silence momentarily separated them once again. Melody could hear the L.A. morning news in the background. A noise in her own back bedroom let her know that Lena was awake. She smiled when she heard her daughter's laughter.

"Look, I have to get Lena up and I am on my way to Indy for a while," Melody said.

"Why, babe? Shouldn't you be home resting? You've been a bit busy and stressed," Tyler said.

"You're right, but since my family has left me no choice but to be the designated survivor, I must do what I have to do," Melody said.

"Are you driving? When are you leaving?" Tyler asked.

"Yes, and in a few hours. I'll be at Mia and Corey's house with Taylor and CJ."

"I'll be home soon, baby. I promise. I just need you not to be mad at me. You are all I have. I can't without you. Do you understand?"

"Yeah, I get it, Tyler."

"Call me when you get to Indy," Tyler requested.

"Okay."

"Promise me," Tyler said.

"Okay, I will call. Bye." She hung up the phone.

Taking a deep breath, Melody fought the urge to call Tyler back and beg him to come home immediately. Her focus now had to be on the children.

"Lena?" Melody called her daughter's name.

"Mom...me. Mom...me," Lena sang

"It's time to brush your teeth and..." Melody's heart jolted to rapid beat.

"Mommy! Mommy! Daddy came to see us." Lena jumped up and down on her bed.

Melody's eyes traveled over her ex sitting in their daughter's bedroom. His scraggly appearance overshadowed what once was a handsome man. His unkempt beard was patchy and she wondered when he shaved last. His crimson eyes watched her nervously.

"Edward, what are you doing here?" Melody stepped closer reaching for the bouncing Lena.

Edward quickly stood and pulled Lena toward him.

"Daddy, you stinky!" Lena giggled and waved her hand under her nose.

"Oh, baby girl, don't break Daddy's heart." Edward smiled and wiped his eyes as if he were crying.

"Okay, Daddy. Sorry," Lena said, wiping his eyes.

"Edward?" Melody's voice shook. Something was wrong. She knew Edward had gone away a few times for therapy, but not once did she think that her ex love could suffer from mental illness.

"What?" Edward asked.

"Are you okay? I… You seem tired," Melody lied. She wanted to say that he looked like a basket case but speaking so frankly would probably cause harm to both her and little Lena.

"Now, see I don't understand why people keep asking me that. I'm perfectly fine." Edward let Lena go and started to pace back and forth.

Sensing awkwardness, Lena quickly ran to her mother. "Daddy okay?"

"Yeah, let's go see Grandma and Grandpa." Melody gently pushed her daughter toward the front door.

"Shut up!" Edward screamed to no one in particular, but his eyes soon focused on Melody. He pulled a switch blade from his pocket and pointed it toward her.

"Run, baby! Go to grandma. Go," Melody screamed.

Lena, unsure of what to do, began to cry. Her sudden sobs unveiled her fear that rooted her little body to the floor.

"What's wrong with you, girl?" Edward grabbed Melody by the throat. "You got my daughter thinking that I'm some damn lunatic off the street. I'm her father. She came from me."

"Edward, this isn't you. What's wrong?" Melody's voice cracked as his grip became tighter.

"Shut up, Melody. You won't trick me this time." Edward's eyes shot daggers.

"Trick you?" Melody whispered.

"Yes, trick me. You put some mind control mess on me. Talking about how Mia doesn't deserve me. You really got me at a low point. I fell for the good stuff last time. I won't again. I'm a shadow of the man that I used to be." The sourness of Edward's breath caused her stomach to turn. His bitterness was eating him from the inside.

"That was a long time ago. We both made a mistake that cost us so much."

"Cost us? You're living in your rich husband's guest house that is twice the size of my parents' home and I'm barely making it in a one room efficiency. Looks like you made it out this mess a whole lot better than me, Melody." Edward shoved her away from him, but still held his knife.

"I'm sorry, Edward. If I could turn back time and erase our mistake then I would, but what is done is done." Melody glanced at her daughter. Guilt hit her. Erasing time would mean Lena would not exist. She did not regret the birth of her daughter.

"Well, you're going to help me make it right."

"How?"

"You don't get to ask questions. Pack a quick bag for Lena and yourself. We're going to take a little road trip."

Melody swallowed. "Edward, I—"

"I said pack a bag." Edward cut off her plea. Reaching for Lena, he pulled the little girl onto his lap. This time Lena wasn't smiling. She watched her mother. Attempting a smile, Melody returned Lena's stare.

"Don't get any ideas. I'm a desperate man with nothing to lose."

"Okay," Melody said.

"Give me your phone." Edward pointed to Melody's mobile device.

Melody grimaced. She was hoping that it would've gone unnoticed. She handed him the phone and turned to leave the room.

"Melody, don't take too long. Five minutes is good enough. We need to leave."

She nodded and avoided eye contact with Lena. The fear on Lena's face was more than enough to push her over the edge. Attacking Edward was not a good move right now. Killing the father of her daughter was something she couldn't live with. At least, not right now.

It was easy to find a bag. She had every intention in grabbing Tyler's gym bag. She needed him at this very instant and if a bag was the last memory she would have of him then so be it. Hubby had chosen to stay and play cops and robbers with America's most wanted and now his family was in jeopardy. Rage swarmed through her as she thought of the entire situation. If Peyton wouldn't have fallen for a bad boy, Tyler would be home. Or better yet, if Edward hadn't appeared to be the catch of a lifetime, then maybe she wouldn't be in this mess. Lusting after her sister's then husband, Edward had turned out to be one of the biggest regrets of her life. Her foolish jealous antics had landed her with a child by Edward and a family torn apart. Hindsight would forever be twenty-twenty. This situation could not get any worse. Furthermore, how did Edward become so mentally imbalanced? How did she not see the signs? Did Mia see them? During their love affair, he would always take a few pills after breakfast, but he claimed they were a vitamin cocktail given to him by his fitness trainer. Funny thing, Melody didn't remember Edward regularly visiting the gym. Nothing would come of thinking on the past.

Melody stuffed clothing in the bag along with a few of Lena's toys and stuffed a few large bills in her bra. If there was ever a moment for she and her baby to escape, then she would take it. Her eyes shifted across the bedroom, Tyler's gun was stashed in a safe in the drawer of their night stand. Listening for movement, Melody quickly reached for the box. She didn't want to shoot Edward, but at this point all that mattered was her daughter.

Melody could feel her heart pound wildly in her chest as she moved her thumb over the combination lock.

"What are you doing?" Edward startled her.

"Nothing."

"It doesn't look like nothing to me." Edward walked in front of her and glanced at the box in front of her.

"It's nothing," Melody lied

"What is it?" Edward asked.

"None of your business. I miss my husband. I wanted to be able to take something with me on this trip to God knows where to do God knows what. It's just a few love letters, Edward. Honestly!" Melody stood to deflect Edward from the box. If she had to open it, she surely would have to shoot him.

"Let's go. If all works out, you and your husband will be together. Maybe we all can sit down and talk once Mia comes to her senses."

"Yeah, maybe." Melody looked at Edward.

"I don't mean to scare you. Let's go."

"Let's go," Melody said, but her feet were rooted to the floor.

Edward watched her and gestured for her to leave the room.

"I need to use the restroom and so does our daughter."

"She didn't say anything about that." Edward frowned.

"At this age, they never do, but you'll be amazed at how a car ride can work on a kid's bladder. Trust me." Melody attempted to smile to lighten the blanket of emotion that seemed to surround them.

"Yeah, I remember that about Taylor." Edward's eyes briefly closed as he thought of his oldest daughter. "Mia use to get so frustrated when Taylor needed to go to the restroom the first ten minutes of a road trip."

"I'll just get Lena and we'll be right out." Melody started walking.

"But, I'm no fool." Edward's eyes popped open. "You go handle your business and I'll make sure Lena gets a chance to go."

"Thank you." Melody gave a terse nod and walked to the master bedroom's bathroom.

Closing the door behind her, Melody quickly reached for her notepad and pen that she had in her vanity drawer. She wrote quickly and prayed someone would find her written plea for help. She had no chance in getting Tyler's gun.

Chapter Eighteen

Why do you see the speck that is in your brother's eye, but do not notice the log that is in your own eye? Or how can you say to your brother, 'Let me take the speck out of your eye,' when there is the log in your own eye? You hypocrite, first take the log out of your own eye, and then you will see clearly to take the speck out of your brother's eye. MATTHEW 7:3-5 ESV

MIA sat in Andrew's office thinking of her sister. The last time they had talked, their words had been rather short because of sister's meddling. After Melody admitted to knowing about Andrew and Los Angeles, there wasn't much point in denying the truth.

Blame could be placed on so many. She could criticize her parents who kept a dirty secret from her for years. Charges could be placed on Melody who had been so jealous that she ended up bedding Edward several times and producing a child. Mia could blame her ex-husband for being an insecure man in search of power. She could even blame Corey for introducing her to the Phillips cartel that made her one of the most sought-after money launderers on the west coast. In the end, she would be a hypocrite in pointing out the faults of others as she crunched numbers for criminal.

Regret rested heavily on the bosom of Mia and her anger ripped the hinges off Pandora's box. Now, she slow danced with the devil while barely missing the edge of an open grave. She had forgiven her family for the pain they had caused her, but she hadn't taken time to pray for the enemies that she left behind nearly three years ago. Mia wondered why she hadn't prayed for Tennessee and the Phillips family. Residue of hatred had hibernated deep within her until it had been violently shaken awake. Asking God to grant them mercy had caused a foul bitterness to brew within her.

The buzz of Mia's phone pulled her from her thoughts. Looking at the screen, Corey had sent a message. A brief smile sat on her lips. He told her that he loved her and that they would meet for dinner at 7:00 p.m.

"Is that beautiful smile for me?" Andrew asked as he entered the room.

"No." Mia didn't lie.

"Wow, you certainly know how to break a man's heart. Since you're making me money, I'll let you slide this time." Andrew walked toward her.

Mia jumped to her feet not wanting Andrew to hover. "I was able to close on a few homes. I think you should be all set. Hopefully, you have someone in mind who can take care of the business."

"I do." Andrew winked.

"Great, because, I'm really looking forward to going back to Indy," Mia said.

"I don't get your rush to return to mediocrity." Andrew shook his head.

"It's not for you to understand, but enough already. Andrew, I'm booking a flight in a few days to return home. It's time Corey and I got back. We've been here far too long," Mia said.

"You're not going anywhere. You are home, dammit." Andrew hit his fist on the table causing a few papers to fall to the floor.

"I have kids and a life. I'm getting ready to have a baby," Mia shot back.

"I can get your children here. Don't worry about that. You're not going back."

"My husband is not going to go for that." Mia's excuse sounded pitiful to her own ears.

"The hell he won't. He's broke and he's back to the place that made him a god. You took him from that." Andrew's eyes traveled over Mia. "And I can definitely see why he left. But he knows where home is. I already have a job for him."

"What? No." Mia walked toward the door but was violently snatched. The pull caused her to fall backward and Andrew placed his foot over her stomach. Mia quickly flipped over to protect her unborn child.

"You're smart. You know what I'm capable of. So, why do you continue to resist? I don't get it. I mean, it's almost breathtaking, the beauty of your resistance," Andrew said as he pulled her from the floor by her hair.

"Get off me." Mia attempted to pull her hair from his hands.

Andrew slapped Mia and she stumbled backwards. Her mouth was agape as she was stunned by his violence.

"Stop resisting." Andrew stepped toward her.

"No!" Mia's natural reaction was to push him. Regret instantly rushed her. Andrew's face twisted, and he barreled toward her like a bull to a red flag. They now played a cat and mouse game around the conference room table.

"Come here," Andrew hollered.

"No, you have absolutely lost your mind. You've put your hands on me. I'm pregnant. This is crazy." Mia ran to the end of the table as Andrew attempted to catch her.

"You're right." Andrew stopped. "I'm not about to chase you." Andrew called to his security team in the hall. "Take Mrs. Phillips home," Andrew said.

"No! No!" Mia cried as two men quickly approached her. Feeling defenseless, she dropped to her knees, but not for long. She was pulled and half carried out of the room. There was nothing really left to say. Life as she knew it was over. Where was God now? Her eyes cast to the ground, a short prayer escaped her lips. She asked God to cover her family as her lower abdomen started cramping.

Corey's jaw clenched as he pulled in front of his father's dope house. The place was different, but the neighborhood was the same. Street soldiers wearing distinct colors stood unapologetic on steps of abandon houses. Their shifty eyes patrolled the streets for cops and searched for addicts.

Disgust clenched Corey's stomach. What once appeared as golden gates to financial freedom now appeared as a rusty old door to hell. Yet, he was back at the king's castle looking for a handout. He told Mia to trust him. He brought her to this mess and he would be the one to bring her out even if it meant he had to resell his soul to the beast. At least he had a taste of what life could've been with the woman he's been in love with for years. The American Dream had been good while it lasted, but in this world, he was just another black man trying to get out.

Hitting his fist on the steering wheel, Corey took a deep breath. He couldn't trust the FEDS to get them out this situation. They wanted to wire his wife and he couldn't put her in jeopardy.

Corey exited the car and looked at the young guy with long dreadlocks standing on the porch. Seeing the guy reminded him of a young K. Swift, his late best friend. Locks nodded and so did Corey.

"What's up? I'm here to see Adrian. I'm—"

"I know who you are. You're a legend," the young man interjected.

"Yeah?" Corey became amused.

"Yeah. I'm going to be just like you when I grow up," he joked.

"Well, if you do, you'll be smarter to know that this isn't what it seems to be," Corey said.

"My name's Cato."

"Cato? Big C's son?" Corey remembered Big C, Cato Sr., making moves in Atlanta years ago. He came to L.A. twenty years ago when a gang took over his territory and threatened to kill his family. Big C left and merged his empire with Adrian. All was well until he killed himself years ago. Cato was a kid at the time when his mother found her husband in the car with his brains splattered and a gun in hand.

"Yes, the one and only." Cato smiled

"Man, I haven't seen you in years."

"Yes, I spent some time upstate."

"Alright, new money, I'll see you around." Corey nodded.

"Good to have you back," Cato said.

Corey walked into the house. A few men sat in the living room watching a large flat screen TV. Guns were scattered on the table along with an ashtray that held burning cigarettes. They briefly glanced at him and continued with their leisure. There was no need for greetings.

Walking past them into the back hallway, Corey knew to head straight to the master bedroom. That's the way it had always been.

"My son." Adrian stood.

"Adrian," Corey replied.

"I'm glad you made it. For a minute, I thought you wouldn't come. You know, get scared and have a coming to Jesus moment." Adrian snickered.

"I'm here." Corey held his tongue. What he wanted to say was that he was now desperate to protect his family and dancing with the devil was not off his plate yet.

"Yes, you are. I knew you'd be back."

"I'm here for my family."

"You're here because you're family," Adrian countered.

"Okay." Corey shrugged.

"So, what is going on with Mia and Andrew?" Adrian gestured for Corey to sit down.

"He's not letting her go and I'm not letting him have her."

"Three years ago you came to the city with that girl. I knew she had your heart the moment she walked in my office. Now, you're ready to knock out one of the most ruthless men in the city." Adrian shook his head and pulled out a cigar.

"Kind of like the way you felt about my mother before you left her." Corey sat down.

Silence entered the room. Adrian took a deep breath and sat, too.

"If that's the case, then I'd be willing to kill a man like Andrew," Adrian said.

"I'm a man that won't let anyone or anything hurt my family," Corey responded.

"Then you're a killer in the making."

"I need to get my wife out of the condo tonight."

"Don't worry about that. I already have someone on the way to get her."

"What about my kids?"

"I sent plane tickets to Jamal. They'll be on the plane day after tomorrow. His mother will be accompanying them. Jamal will be locking your house down."

"Tennessee?"

"Let me worry about him."

"So, what's it going to cost me?"

"Son, I could never charge you a dime." Adrian smiled.

"You know what I mean, Pop." Corey was in no mood for games.

"I'm ready for you to come back to the winning side, the dream team, son. I can't run this empire forever. You're the last man standing."

"The last pick, huh?"

"You got it all wrong, son. You proved Darwin's theory."

"What?"

"Survival of the fittest. You're still here after all this."

"God got me through this, not some dude named Darwin."

"Yeah? Did he now? Because you're here now and my name is not God." Adrian smirked.

"Look, I'll do what I gotta do."

"Then first things first. Once I give word to get rid of Andrew, I want you with me when I put a bullet in the head of Tennessee. I might even let you pull the trigger, son."

"I'm not shooting anyone." Corey nostrils flared.

"We'll see." Adrian winked. "Look, I got a meeting in a few. Take a run with Cato. There's some new fools in town trying to take a few of our regulars. Check them."

Corey fought the urge to knock his father's head through a wall.

"Before you leave, take this with you." Adrian tossed at least twenty hundred dollar bills on the table.

"What's this?" Corey asked.

"A little pocket change. I know it's been a while since you've seen that many Franklins. It's like riding a bike, son. Go slow, you'll remember." Adrian started laughing.

Corey hesitated before grabbing the money as he knew it sealed the deal.

Life as he knew it was over as he walked outside. Cato was already sitting in the driver's side of a clean, late model sedan with tinted windows. The windows were down and the loud explicit pulsed through the air.

As soon as Corey sat down, he turned the music off.

"What's up, man? You not feeling Sir KayLo?" Cato asked.

Corey wondered if Cato would have thought him to be crazy if he asked if they could listen to some gospel music while on the way to do a possible drive by.

"I'm just not feeling any music right now," Corey lied.

"Anything you say, boss." Cato smiled.

Glancing at the young man, Corey quirked his eyebrows at the boss comment.

"What? You are the man now. Adrian has made it clear that you're back and running things as if you never left."

"Really? What do you know about me leaving?"

"Word is that you did it for love. Lady came down here and knocked you off your feet and you left it all behind. Hood fairytale." Cato smiled.

"Something like that."

Chapter Nineteen

Vindicate me, O God, and defend my cause against an
ungodly people, from the deceitful and unjust man deliver me!
PSALM 43:1 ESV

TYLER left another voicemail for his wife. He hadn't talked to her
in several hours and he was beginning to worry. His calls were
going straight to voicemail and she hadn't answered any of his text
messages. He resisted the urge to call his father. Involving him in this
would only anger the great Charles. But if he didn't hear from her in
an hour, he would be calling everyone.

Taking a deep breath, Tyler picked up his phone again and this
time dialed his sister-in-law.

"Tyler," Mia answered.

"Hey, Mia. How are you?"

"I guess as good as I can be under the circumstances."

"Yeah, I know what you mean, Mia. I'm sorry about all this."

"Hmmm, are you, Tyler?" Mia asked.

"Am I what?" Tyler was taken aback by her response.

"Sorry about all this? You know what I mean."

"Okay?" Tyler countered.

"I don't have a choice in being in this nightmare. And you, Tyler,
have a choice. You can be with your family in Chicago right now. But

you have my sister about to have a breakdown worrying about you and trying to bring happiness into a marriage full of a lot of pain and suffering."

"Mia, you're overstepping yourself." Tyler could feel his heart pound in his ears.

"No, I'm not. Don't you get it?" Mia's voice cracked. "I'm not coming home. The life that I thought I had will never be the same. I can't come back and you're here jeopardizing my sister's life. Who will she have if we're both gone, Tyler?"

"I... Mia, you just don't get it."

"Get on a plane. And go to my sister."

"I haven't heard from her. I keep calling. She isn't answering."

"What?" Mia screamed through the phone.

"When was the last time you talked to her?"

"Yesterday. Why aren't you on a plane right now? Get out of here and go find her. If you let anything happen to my sister, so help me..."

"Look—"

"No, you look. You're chasing Peyton's killer and somebody could be hurting my sister and my niece. You can't bring Peyton back, but you can do something about your family that is still living."

"You sound like Melody."

Tyler could hear someone knocking at Mia's door on the other end of the line.

"Then there's your confirmation. Why... did ....you call me, Tyler?" Mia became a bit distracted.

"It doesn't matter," Tyler said.

"Don't worry about Andrew. He'll pay for his crime. Take care of my sister. Don't call me until you hear from my sister," Mia whispered as she hung up the phone.

The echo of Tyler's frustrating growl could be heard throughout the floor of the hotel. Fear shot through him like lightning bolts. "Pey, I'm sorry, baby sister. I love you, but I have to protect my wife and child," Tyler whispered. "Forgive me Father."

Tyler pulled his bible from the table and eyed the familiar book. God hadn't crossed Tyler's mind in a while. When had he become a hypocrite, he wondered. He stood before the people of Green

Pastures and spoke of God's grand mercies and how God was a champion for the righteous. Yet, Tyler was willing to sacrifice his faith and replace God with his own will to vindicate his sister.

His love for Peyton had been diminished by self loathe. He hated himself for not seeing Peyton's pain while falling in love with Melody. It hurt to know that God had given him a help-mate while painfully removing a part of him. He was loving another woman while Peyton had suffocated in her own blood. Now his mother, too, marked with grief and full of meds, lay in the bed rotting.

Losing Melody and Lena was not an option. He would never be the same and no one would ever be able to replace the love that had been specially designed for him. He'd put everyone at risk including himself to end a man. Andrew gasping for air and bending in pain could never amount to satisfying love of his wife or a chance at eternal life with God.

Tyler turned to Psalm 43 and whispered, "Vindicate me, O God, and defend my cause against an ungodly people, from the deceitful and unjust man deliver me. For you are the God in whom I take refuge; why have you rejected me? Why do I go about mourning because of the oppression of the enemy? Send out your light and your truth; let them lead me; let them bring me to your holy hill and to your dwelling! Then I will go to the altar of God, to God my exceeding joy, and I will praise you with the lyre, O God, my God."

There was no time to pack belongings. Tyler grabbed his wallet and went to the airport. He prayed he wasn't too late.

Mia watched as three men who introduced themselves as friends of Adrian scanned the condo for taps and surveillance. They barely spoke as they pulled several audio transmitters from hidden locations in the house. They looked like federal agents, but she knew better. There was no way a government agency could be in cahoots with the likes of Adrian.

"It's clear, Mia. You have about five minutes to grab what you can before Andrew knows something is not right. Move fast." One of the men gestured through dark shades.

Mia pictured herself in some thriller movie and quickly moved through the condo putting items into her suitcase. The room started to spin as she wondered the purpose of taking anything at all. Once again, her life was in shambles and she wondered why God had put her under the oppression of her enemy.

"I'm ready." Mia stood with her purse.

"That's all?"

"Yeah, where is Corey? Who has my children?" Mia asked.

"You'll see them soon. Let's go."

Mia was hustled into an awaiting black SUV, but not before she saw a car approaching.

"We have company," one of the men spoke.

"Yeah, I see that, D," the driver responded.

"Reggie, get ready. We don't know who this is and we really don't want to stick around to find out," D responded.

"Why don't we just pull off now?" Mia's heart was about to pop out of her chest.

"We don't want to have a car chase on our hands, Mia. That would bring a lot of unnecessary attention. Just keep calm. Be quiet," D said, tucking his gun in his waistband and stepping from the car.

A dark sedan pulled in front of the condo and a woman stepped from the vehicle. Her appealing frame was donned in a knee length gray skirt and matching jacket. A visible badge was hooked on her waist. Her tight bun did not take away from her attractive features and her no nonsense expression said she was on a mission.

"Could this get any worse?" Mia mumbled.

"No worries. Just pay attention." Reggie smiled and pointed toward D and the woman.

Mia strained to listen to their conversation through the door D had left open.

"Melanie." D smiled.

"Dwayne. What are you doing here?" Melanie asked as she pulled her sunglasses from her eyes.

"Doing my job. What else?" Dwayne smirked. "Agent Stevens, always so serious. The hottie of the bureau. When are you going to let your hair down and let me take you out?"

"When I die, you may take me out. Now, you didn't answer my

132

question." Melanie set her eyes on the car causing Mia to sink in her seat.

"Relax, she can't see in this car," Reggie whispered.

"Like I said, I'm doing my job and I don't have to answer to you. I answer to the DEA and you are not the DEA," Dwayne said.

"Okay. Well, I'll ask this then, Agent Dwayne. Did you find what you're looking for at this property?"

"No." Dwayne shook his head. "I was sent to question a guest staying at this house. No one's home."

"Really? Mind if I check?" Melanie asked.

"Go ahead." Dwayne gestured toward the house. "In the meantime, I have places to be. Call me tonight, Melanie. I'm free."

"See you later, Dwayne." Melanie rolled her eyes.

Dwayne turned and got in the car. "Let's go."

Reggie didn't hesitate as he drove off. Mia was relieved to be out of the presence of Melanie. Some official agency was looking for her. Now she was on the run from the law and a crazed criminal. Yet, her rescue team consisted of a corrupt DEA agents and a drug lord. From the pan to the fire.

"Are you taking me to my husband?"

"Lady, you ask a lot of questions." D frowned as he pulled out his phone.

Mia decided against responding. She was grateful that she didn't have to deal with whatever was coming her way with Melanie. She wanted to be in the arms of her husband and touch the faces of her children.

Chapter Twenty

Pray without ceasing. Thessalonians 5:17 ESV

MELODY sat in her sister's bedroom with a terrified Taylor, a nervous Lena, and an oblivious baby CJ. Hours ago, Edward forced Melody to call her parents and a lie about a pop in visit with the children. Her mother had been ecstatic about her daughter's surprise visit and allowed Taylor and CJ to stay home from midweek service to spend time with their aunt and cousin. Edward took advantage of the opportunity and added more hostages.

Melody searched the room for a weapon for what seemed like the hundredth time. The idea of hurting her baby daddy made her queasy, but she chose the lives of the children who desperately needed her to be the stronger and wiser person in the room.

They all watched as Edward pulled Corey's clothing from the closet and tossed them to the floor. Edward was mumbling to himself, but what she could pull from his mumbling was that it was time for Corey to go. Melody was grateful when Edward left the room to get a garbage bag

"Aunt Melody?" Taylor whispered.

"Yes, baby," Melody said.

"What is wrong with Dad?" Taylor asked. "He's acting crazy."

"I'm not exactly sure," Melody lied. Edward had lost his mind and now committing a felony. At least she hoped it would end with him just kidnapping them. Anything else would end in murder.

"I'm scared." Taylor frowned. "I want my mom and Corey."

Melody watched CJ roll around in his pack and play. He seemed content with his bottle and toys, but yet Melody feared for him the most. Taylor and Lena were Edward's biological children, but CJ was Corey's child. She didn't miss the look of fury that Edward had given the baby after tossing him in the playpen.

"Don't be afraid. I won't let anything happen to you. I need to get to a phone," Melody said.

"Dad has my phone."

"A tablet or a laptop?" Melody was desperate.

"My tablet is in the kitchen."

"That will be hard to get." Melody sighed.

"Wait, my old phone is in Corey's office."

"Is it still working?" Melody asked.

"I don't know. But can we try?" Taylor eyed the hallway.

Melody thought about it and wondered if it was worth the effort. She was not willing to involve the children if there was even a small possibility of getting caught.

"Let's just wait. I…" Melody stopped when Edward stood in the doorway.

"Y'all hungry? I ordered pizza." Edward looked at them until his gaze rested uncomfortably on little CJ.

Melody quickly grabbed her nephew and pulled him close. "I'm sure the children are hungry."

"That big old boy eating table food yet?" Edward muttered.

"He's a baby." Melody gestured for Lena and Taylor to get up.

Taylor noticed Edward's uneasiness toward CJ and quickly walked toward Melody.

"This is my brother." Taylor rested her hand on CJ's leg causing the baby to give her a gummy smile.

"Yeah? The last time I checked, I didn't have any kids to give you a brother," Edward said.

"Edward! Stop," Melody demanded as Taylor pulled Lena close.

"What? No one told Mia to go mess around with some thug and have his baby." Edward walked toward Melody and turned CJ's face toward his.

"You could have been mine, but your mom, but I…" Edward whispered.

"Don't touch him. Don't talk to him. Don't even look at him." Melody backed away.

"What?" Edward snarled.

"Daddy don't hurt my mommy!" Lena forced her little body between both her parents.

Shaking his head back and forth, Edward loosed himself from his psychotic thoughts. His clenched fist relaxed and the tick in his jaw calmed.

"Daddy's sorry, baby." Edward got on his knees to pull Lena close.

"Don't hurt Mommy. Don't hurt Taylor. Don't hurt CJ. Don't hurt me," Lena cried.

"Oh, I won't do anything to upset you." Edward scooped her up and began walking down the steps.

Fingers twitching, Melody eyed the lamp in the hallway. This would have been the perfect opportunity to pick it up and bash it across Edward's head to make an escape, but he was holding their daughter. He'd been smart. If she hurt him while holding their daughter, he would have time to hurt Lena.

Feeling a pull on her hand, Melody turned to find Taylor nodding her head toward Corey's office. Melody mouthed no, but Taylor let go of her hand and quietly walked away.

"Where are you going?" Edward asked, startling Melody and Taylor.

"Dad, I have to pee. I haven't gone since we've been on the road," Taylor barked.

"Alright, baby girl. We'll wait." Edward remained planted.

"Are you serious? I mean really, Dad? What can I do?" Taylor nearly shrieked.

"Alright, baby. But don't take too long. I don't want your pizza to get cold." Edward smiled, and Taylor scowled.

"She's feisty. Seems like Corey is trying to take my place," Edward murmured.

Adrenaline pulsed through Melody so hard, she could feel it push through her veins. She was going to have to hurt this man in order to be set free. Plots and scenarios of hurting her ex-lover reeled through her mind like a blotchy horror film.

"No one is taking your place." Melody wondered if she was telling the truth. Corey hadn't taken the place of Edward. Perhaps Edward had taken the place of Corey. Mia was head over heels in love with Corey and her heart had been shattered in a million pieces when he'd left to live with his father. Mia had come home from school crying when she'd been told that he left to go to California. Remembering her sister's heart wrenching sobs, Melody remembered her mother comforting her older sister. A couple of years later, Mia had come home from college with Edward who soon became her fiancé. He was alright, but Melody was surprised when Mia actually married him. They'd made a pack right after Mia's high school graduation they would catch a plane to Los Angeles and get her man. Mia was set on using her part time job money for two tickets to Los Angeles. Somehow the plan was lost.

"You sure about that?" Edward asked.

"What I'm sure about is that you're making a huge mistake, Edward," Melody said.

"Shut up. Shut. Up," Edward screamed. Lena jerked and twisted her body from Edward and ran to her mother.

"Edward," Melody called.

"No!" Edward charged toward Melody.

Moving quickly Melody placed CJ into the flimsy little arms of Lena.

"Lena, go to Taylor!" Melody pushed her daughter away just in time as calloused hands wrapped around her neck.

Melody could hear the horrified screams of Lena, but Edward's power overshadowed the pleas of her daughter. She slapped at his hands, but the more she grabbed the more the air left her. The room began to spin and she stared into the red eyes at the demon that distorted Edward's sweaty face. Cakey white foam sat in the corners of his mouth as he shouted curses.

Melody wanted to speak but couldn't form the words. A prayer of mercy played in her thoughts.

God, protect the children. Let no harm come to them. Forgive Edward. Let Tyler be set free from my death. Don't let him blame himself for my death. If it is Your will, save me, God. I will pray without ceasing. I will call You until my last breath.

Melody continued her prayer as her hands began to loosen from Edward's death grip. Just as darkness started to take over, she felt the collapse of Edward. Another thump and he lay very still beside her.

Her own coughing and gasps burned her throat.

"Aunt Melody?" Taylor cried as she held the end of a bloody table lamp in her hand. Her knuckles were nearly white as she gripped the light. She hoped the blow that Taylor delivered was not fatal, but right now she was also grateful for her own life.

Melody grabbed her throat and whispered. "Get the kids. We're getting out of here." Melody pulled her body into a standing position.

Taylor ran to the room and moments later returned with two wide eyed children. Immediately CJ reached for Melody and she pulled him close. Lena stared at her father.

"We have to go," Melody said.

"No, we have to finish this." Taylor stood over Edward's lifeless body.

"What?" Melody said.

"I mean, he tried to kill you. Are you crazy? Stupid? He... He's not going to try to do it again. I am not going through this with you. He's going to hurt CJ. I could see it in his eyes, Aunt Melody." Taylor's voice cracked.

Shuffling CJ to her side, Melody grabbed Taylor's arm.

"I don't want to hear you say that ever again."

"What? Why? He's crazy. He wants Mama back. I know I was young when all that stuff happened between y'all, but I wasn't stupid. I was hurt, too. And now... Now, he's trying to hurt my mom again, by causing all this... I'm going to kill him," Taylor screamed.

"Vengeance is mine said the Lord." Melody pulled Taylor close.

Taylor yanked away. "Then why is my mom back in California if God is supposed to be avenging people, huh? Huh?"

"How did you know your mom is in California?" Melody asked.

"Why do you all keep thinking I'm stupid? Let's just go." Taylor rolled her eyes.

"I have to call the police. Take CJ. Get in Corey's car."

"Yeah, whatever." Taylor took CJ and walked away.

Melody ignored Taylor's attitude. The girl had been traumatized. They all had been.

Edward's fingers twitched and Melody wondered if Taylor had hit him too hard. Pushing her foot into his side, she hoped for a moan. There was nothing.

"Lord, let this man live," she whispered as she pulled her phone from his pocket to call the police.

"Nine-one-one operator. What is your emergency?"

"I... Sorry, false alarm," Melody stammered.

"Ma'am, are you okay? Are you unable to talk?" the operator asked.

"I'm fine. False alarm. My house alarm was triggered when my daughter hit a ball through the glass. My apologies," Melody lied before hanging up.

If the police came, they would ask questions and she wasn't willing to give the whereabouts of her sister and brother-in-law and jeopardize them or even worse get their children taken away. Everything would be exposed, and a scandal would break with Tyler. Melody wanted to scream. Picking up the phone, she dialed another number.

"Hello?"

"Daddy?"

"What's wrong, baby?" Michael's voice expressed immediate concern.

"Tyler is in L.A. trying to avenge Peyton's death. Mia and Corey are in L.A. working for a criminal. Edward kidnapped Lena and I and brought us here to Indy. He then held Taylor and CJ hostage along with us. Taylor bashed Edward across the head with a lamp. He's not moving much, and I can't call the police." Melody unloaded on her father. There was no time to waste.

"Where are you now?" Michael asked.

"I'm at Mia's house."

"Where's Edward?"

"I'm in front of him. The kids are outside."

"Get out the house. I'll be there in a minute. Wait for me in the driveway in the car with the doors locked and the car running." Michael hung up the phone.

Relief washed over her but was soon replaced by a strong bout of nausea and abdominal pain.

Chapter Twenty-One

Now when they heard this they were cut to the heart, and said to Peter and the rest of the apostles, "Brothers, what shall we do?" Acts 2:37 ESV

NAUSEA bubbled in the pit of Corey's stomach and a bitter bile sat on his tongue like stagnant water making him spit on the pavement. He'd just pulled a gun on a man that was old enough to be his father. Terror was the only thing that could describe what was written on the older man's sweaty face as he stared down the barrel of a gun. The image would forever be imprinted in his mind. Bingo was the old man's street name and he just opened up shop to hustle the neighborhood. The man had no intention of trying to take customers from Adrian. He'd only wanted to get a bit of extra money to pay some of his wife's piling medical bills. Bingo had run a corner grocery mart. He'd taken a second loan from the bank to help cover his wife's treatments. He was having a hard time keeping up with the payments. His grandson mentioned an alternative. After a few months of pondering and no money, he gave the streets a try. In one month, he's paid the ten-grand back to the bank. Bingo's love for the quick paper hadn't stopped. Hence the name, Bingo.

"Bro, you crazy, man!" Cato laughed high from adrenaline.

Corey said nothing as he tucked his gun in his waistband. Usually he would secure his gun before leaving, but he wanted to send a message to anybody who thought the Phillips's cartel was playing games. Phillips' cartel had closed Bingo's street candy shop and would immediately be returning to selling overpriced groceries.

"A legend, man. I swear, dude. You were so cool with it. You know what I'm saying. Hesitation. Never. Bingo, trying to take over. Man, you sent a powerful message. Adrian gonna be cool with this," Cato said.

"Yeah?" Corey took a deep breath still remembering Bingo's frozen tears as he begged for his life.

Corey wasn't going to kill him. Even if he wanted to do it, he wouldn't have been able. All the bullets were stuffed in his back pocket. He wasn't a killer and he wouldn't compromise his murder free track record, even for his blood thirsty father.

A cross oddly sat on Bingo's office wall which continued to draw Corey's attention through the entire ordeal. He kept feeling as if God was whispering for him to stop. Corey's spirit begged him to stop, but his flesh could only feel rage.

"This is crazy. Corey is back. Just like old times. Taking care of business. Leaving no question unanswered. You was like, Bingo you have until midnight to shut it down! And at 12:01, if I even feel like you trying to sell anything that is not on the shelves of this rat hole, I'm gonna burn this place down with you in it."

Beads of sweat popped on Corey's forehead. He was ready to pop and throwing up in front of the watching neighborhood would be a sign of weakness.

"Cato, stay right here. I'll be right back." Corey jogged toward a nearby alley.

"You good?" Cato called after him.

Waving the young man off, Corey locked eyes with his target. A dumpster midway through the alley was the perfect place.

As he reached it, disgust in the form of putrid chunks plopped on the ground in a puddle at his feet. His Aunt Zay said conviction could knock an upright man on his knees. He was convicted.

"Why God? My family. I need my wife and my children," Corey said before spewing again.

A cool breeze rushed past him, pulling him back into the reality of his surroundings. He slowly lifting his head and braced himself against the wall. A raspy cough brought his attention to a homeless man quietly watching him. The ragged man sat cross legged in dirty clothing on cardboard. His disheveled appearance did not deflect from the cool stare that he gave Corey.

"You look like you need a drink." The man held an amber colored bottle toward him.

"Naw, I don't drink." Corey wiped the corners of his mouth.

"Yeah, me neither," the man mumbled and put the bottle down.

Corey wondered if the man was crazy for offering a drink if he, himself, didn't.

"I ain't crazy. I keep it so people will think I am. You know. They'll feel sorry for me or think I'm some old drunk, you know, but I see. I see it all." The man laughed.

"I guess you're smart, then." Corey smirked.

"No. I'm stupid. I used to be a quick thinker, but look at me now. I got nothing, but these here eyes and a voice. I guess you done shutdown Bingo. It's for his own good. He don't know nothing about selling other than it gets you money. He didn't take in consideration the politics of it all. Serves him right. He forgot about faith. When his wife, Doris, took ill and he spent money on all them pills to get her better, he left faith out the equation."

"Man, how do you know all this? What's your name?" Corey was grateful for the conversation. It took his mind off his bleak situation.

"My name is Homie." The man gave him a toothless grin.

"Homie?"

"Yeah, I'm the homie of the streets."

Corey shook his head at the old school word. "Okay, Homie."

"Like I said, I know a lot. Like I know this here what you doing, ain't you. It may have been you once before, but it sho' ain't now."

"I can't argue with that, man."

"Then what you waiting for?"

"Too much at stake."

"Can't nothing be that much at stake, for you to be doing what you doing. Once these streets get a hold of you, you'll forget yourself. Too many young men like you lose yourselves to this money. It's like the devil done disguised himself like a big bag of money that says free. Everybody jumps for it. As soon as you land, you done hopped on a cactus. You'll be pulling thorns out your butt for years. "

"I'm not looking for money. I'm looking for safety," Core said.

"Same thing. It's all a trap. It's all a disguise. Gotta have some faith and some smarts."

"What about you? It's doesn't look like things worked out for you," Corey shot back.

"I've made my peace. I know where I'm going. Don't let the looks fool you. The penny in my pocket is worth more than the bills in yours. It's all I got and I won't sell my soul to get another one, but you ready to let the devil buy yours."

"So, what should I do now?" Corey asked.

"End it before—" Police sirens interrupted Homie.

Slamming doors and loud voices could be heard demanding someone to put their hands on the steering wheel.

"Looks like your friend is about to go down." Homie nodded toward the entrance of the alley.

"No!" Corey could feel his heart pound in his chest as he saw Cato's body slammed to the pavement. The cops were asking were the rest of his thug friends were.

"Yeah, you best get out of here. It won't take long before someone starts talking. Back door to the building is open. Go down the stairs and turn left. Keep going until you see a gate. That will put you out front on the other side," Homie said.

"Why are you helping me, old man?" Corey asked.

"Somethin' is telling me that you're different. Now git! Ain't no time for talk."

Corey ran. He needed to get to his family. Pulling out his phone, he called Adrian. He needed to get back on the other side of town. Memories from the past flashed through his mind. This was the same mess, just a different scenario. When Swift went down three years ago, Corey called his father. Now, he was calling again. Cato wasn't dead, but that young dude wouldn't last too long in police custody without whistling.

"Is it done?" Adrian asked.

"Yes, but...we got a problem," Corey spoke, attempting to catch his breath.

"What?"

"Cato just got picked up by the police," Corey said.

"That kid is going to sing. Damn! Go to the Chop house. I got to pack up here. We have to go."

"Where is Mia?" Corey asked.

"She'll be there. Stay low. Everything is cool." Adrian hung up the phone.

Corey had made it to the other side of the building. Now it was time to go unnoticed and get to the Chop House that was a good hike across town.

Chapter Twenty-Two

Let all bitterness and wrath and anger and clamor and slander be put away from you, along with all malice. EPHESIANS 4:31 ESV

TYLER felt a sense of relief as he exited the plane. Finally, he made it to Chicago. His flight had been turbulent from the moment the plane entered the air. If his mind hadn't been so much on Melody, he would have been gripping the edge of the seat like most of the other passengers. The pilot had reassured them that the choppiness was due to high winds and rising air, but that meant nothing to the hundred plus nervous passengers. They just wanted the turbulence to stop and all Tyler wanted was to see his wife. The flight very much reminded him of the present state of his life—topsy turvy.

It didn't take long for Tyler to spot his driver awaiting him in the thick crowd. Jack was the longtime family chauffeur. His prompt professionalism made him a family favorite. Today, Jack held a look of concern.

"Hey, Jack. How are you?" Tyler handed the man his carryon bag. He liked carrying his own luggage but Jack insisted.

"Sir." Jack nodded. "We have a situation."

"What?" Tyler asked.

"Melody and Lena were kidnapped."

Air was sucked from Tyler's lungs as he processed the bad news.

"What?" Tyler shouted, causing a few heads to turn.

"They are fine now, but they are in Indianapolis. Edward forced them by gunpoint," Jack said.

"I need to get to Melody. Is our plane ready?" Tyler asked.

"Yes, we have been cleared to take off on the private runway in 30 minutes. We need to move." Jack started walking.

"Does Melody have her phone? How can I reach her?" Tyler asked

"I...you...you can reach her through her father." Jack hesitated.

"What's the problem?" Tyler couldn't handle anymore upsetting news without punching a hole in the wall.

"Ms. Melody is in the hospital. I don't know anything else. Her father won't say anymore. He said that he would see you when you get there."

Tyler's temper escalated.

Fury pricked Melody as she lay in the hospital bed. Done is what she felt as she stared blankly at the television. Her private luxury room and special treatment meant nothing to comfort the emotional pain.

"Melody, you're going to have to try and eat something." Michelle pointed to the untouched steak and potato dinner.

"I'm not hungry, Mom." Melody willed herself not to roll her eyes.

"You think you're not hungry because hurt is filling you up," Michelle said.

"After the issue with Mia, I never thought I could feel as much hurt again, but I was wrong. Dead wrong." Melody wiped at her eyes. "This hurts too much. I can't come back from this."

"Yes, you can. You're vindicated by God's grace and mercy. This soon shall pass," Michelle said.

"I don't know. I'm tired of passing through. Seems like this is payback for the hell I caused."

"I don't think so. You've repented. That chapter in your life has been over."

"Maybe," Melody responded.

The door to the hospital room opened. "It's time, Mrs. Deen." The tall nurse gave an empathetic smile.

"How long will this take?" Michelle gave a weak smile.

"The actual procedure will take no more than 15 minutes. She'll be in the recovery room within the hour. We'll bring her right back here. She'll more than likely be released tomorrow."

"Okay." Michelle nodded and gently kissed her daughter's head.

Soon, Melody watched the passing lights as she was wheeled away. Voices could be heard around her, but she refused to put a face to the sounds. She wanted no one to see the abyss of emptiness that threatened to take over what life remained in her.

"Okay." The nurse signaled their arrival in the operating room.

Light and pleasant music played in the background and a doctor leaned over her to smile as the nurse checked machines and busied herself with preparations.

Swallowing, Melody tried to remain calm. She'd never experienced a medical procedure that called for her to be put under anesthesia.

"Alright, we need you to move onto the bed here. Nice and easy." The nurse used a reassuring voice.

Melody nodded. She thought of Tyler. He didn't know and wouldn't be here for her. He was too busy in California attempting to pursue his deep rooted passion in avenging Peyton.

"Melody, I'm Dr. Hill. I'm the anesthesiologist. I'll be administering your general anesthesia. You'll be fine." The man smiled.

Everyone seemed to be smiling.

"Alright," Melody said. She was secured on the slab. It didn't take long.

"Okay. Melody, I'm administering the anesthesia through your IV You'll be done in no time."

Melody nodded. Thoughts of Tyler passed through her mind. He was holding her. She was pushing him away. Melody heard the music playing in the background. Her eyes closed.

"Mom?" Tyler walked into his wife's hospital room carrying a dozen fresh cut roses. Disappointment passed through him as he noticed his weary looking mother-in-law watching the evening news.

"Tyler." Michelle stood and gave him a hug.

"Where is Melody?" Tyler asked.

Michelle looked at the clock on the wall. "She should be in the recovery room and probably on her way here, soon."

"Recovery room?" Tyler's heart pounded his chest.

"Melody said she told you." Michelle appeared to be uncomfortable.

"Told me what?" Tyler asked.

"Tyler... I..." Michelle stuttered. "Melody had a miscarriage. She had to get a D&C. The doctor said it was probably due to ongoing stress in her life and well, this latest incident was the icing on the cake."

"She was pregnant?" Tyler sat.

"She didn't know. Approximately nine weeks or so," Michelle said.

"I can't believe this." Tyler rubbed his face.

"I can't either, but now we need to get through this. There are a lot of unanswered questions," Michelle said.

"Right now, I'm not really sure if I'm ready to discuss all of this." He wasn't ready to discuss his crusade or let his mother-in-law know that her other daughter was working for a killer. It was all too incriminating and surreal.

"It doesn't matter if you're ready or not. All of you all's actions have ended in disaster and now you're involving my grandchildren. Three of them were just kidnapped and one lost his life."

Michelle's words cut. His unborn child was dead and his daughter had been subjected to Edward's psychosis. Edward. "Where's Edward?"

"Michael contacted his parents. He's on his way to a facility and will be under close observation."

"Close observation? That man needs to be in jail." Tyler slammed his fist on the wall.

"Calm down. Edward is unstable. He killed someone to get to Melody and Mia. He most definitely will go to jail or some mental hospital for a long time. That's the least of your worries. That case is closed. I feel sorry for the man who lost his life and the family he unwillingly left behind. Yet, your family was spared while you were running around California playing cops and robbers," Michelle snapped.

"I'm here now," Tyler said.

"Why are you here now?" Melody asked as she was wheeled in the room.

An uncomfortable silence filled the room as she was assisted into the bed. The medical attendant wasted no time in leaving.

"Baby." Tyler stood and touched Melody's face.

She looked away. "I asked you, why are you here?"

"What do you mean? I'm your husband. I'm supposed to be here," Tyler said.

"Oh, now you want to be here? I'm so done." Melody shook her head.

"Done?" Tyler asked.

"DONE! DONE! OVER! I want a divorce."

"Melody! You're overreacting," Michelle exclaimed.

"Yeah? Good. I should've been overreacting a lot sooner. It gets results." Melody fumed.

"We're not getting a divorce." Tyler wanted to punch a hole in the wall.

"Get out, Tyler. I've already contacted my lawyer. I was cool until I lost my baby because of you. I've been wanting a family, but I've been busy taking care of your past. I can't do this with you. Get out! Get out!"

"We're not getting a divorce. I'm not losing you, but I'm going to give you some space. I'll be here to pick you up when you get discharged." Tyler attempted a calm voice although his heart was breaking.

"Tyler, Lena is with Michael," Michelle said.

"I'm going to get all the kids. We're going out to eat or something. Melody, I love you. I'll see you tomorrow." Tyler walked out.

Tears burned the back of his eyes. He wanted to run back in the room and talk some sense into her and beg for forgiveness. He messed up, but what they had was not to be thrown away. Their vows included for better or worse. His thoughts made him feel like a hypocrite. He didn't want his wife to throw their relationship away, but he'd done the same when he wouldn't let go.

"God, fix me and my wife. Let all the bitterness, wrath, anger, and malice be put away from her." Tyler prayed as he walked away.

Chapter Twenty-Three

"Refrain from anger, and forsake wrath! Fret not yourself; it tends only to evil." PSALM 37:8 ESV

ANDREW had called Mia's phone at least a dozen times within the last couple of hours. He even sent a bone chilling text: *If you're not dead, you're going to wish you were.* After the threatening text, Adrian threw her phone into a tub of water to lose the signal. Now she and her father-in-law sat on the deck watching the sun go down. Streaks of yellow gold and burnt orange streaked the sky as the sun seemed to slowly disappear into the hills.

"When will Corey get here?" Mia asked.

"Soon. He had to lay low. That takes time. Don't worry." Adrian propped his feet on the stool in front of him.

"I'm not worried. I'm just ready for this to end." Mia fought the urge to push Adrian from his carefree disposition. She felt like a hypocrite relaxing in the sunset with a man who wanted to kill her less than three years ago. Now she was at the mercy of his protection or so Corey thought.

"Do you think that once Corey gets here, you'll go back to your cute little life?" Adrian smirked.

"I don't know. I just know that I don't want to be here with you selling dope to innocent people," Mia shot back.

"Innocent people?" Adrian laughed. "Look, trust me when I say this, people are searching for answers to their problems. Life has no friends. Life and death have a love/hate relationship. There is no one without the other and they argue all the time."

"Your point?" Mia asked.

"My point is that in this life, Mia, people have struggles. Some people search for help at church and others search for answers elsewhere. I'm one of those alternative answers in the elsewhere," Adrian said.

"Really? Huge difference." Mia threw her hands in the air.

"You got pastors up here taking half your paycheck and you still have the same problems you had when you came to church. As a matter of fact, you got more problems because now you can't pay your bills. Church talking about having faith and you sitting in the dark feeding your kids grilled cheese on moldy bread. Then when you get to church, it's a holy fashion show. Problem is that you can't afford new clothes because you gave five offerings in thirty minutes and the pastor is wearing your check. Stupid." Adrian was now looking at her.

"Sounds like you've been hurt," Mia said.

"Naw. I'm no fool, but they got my wife and she died broke trying to raise four kids." Adrian hissed.

"When she was raising them, they were happy and they were alive. Then you got them. One is dead. The other is locked up. One won't speak to you or even of you. And you got my husband who is close to despising you. And they weren't broke. Had you taken some time to see about them and respect your wife, you would've known that she never went without."

"Woman, who do you think you are talking to?" Adrian stood and so did Mia.

"I'm talking to you. The man who wanted me dead. The man who has made the man I love consider coming back to work for you in order to protect his family. The man who hates God because of his own shortcomings."

"I swear if you weren't my son's wife, I'd hit you in your mouth." Adrian stepped closer.

"And I swear if you weren't my husband's father and my children's grandfather, I'd bash your head in with this chair," Mia screamed.

Adrian's demeanor quickly changed from enraged to amused. "Well, at least I know you're a fighter. Sit down. We don't have time for this. Our opinions differ, but trust that right now, I'm your only option because out there is either death or prison. And ain't no church or god gonna keep them streets off your back," Adrian said before sitting down.

Mia sat down as well. She refused to allow Adrian to take her to the sunken place when she first met him. Back then she had given up on God.

"Baby." Corey called to his wife as he walked on the deck.

Immediately, Mia went into his arms for comfort. His breathing and scent calmed her.

"Corey, I'm so glad to see you," Mia whispered.

Corey kissed her forehead. "I'm so glad to see you. How are you feeling? How's our baby?" He touched her stomach.

"We're fine." Mia noticed Adrian looking at them with a mix of admiration and regret.

"Have you heard from Cato?" Corey asked his father.

"I sent a lawyer to him. All is good. They have nothing to hold him on. But, I still want him out of there. They should be releasing him soon," Adrian said.

"Good," Corey said. "Look, Mia needs some rest and she needs a doctor. She's missed her appointment."

"Yeah, I can handle that. In the mean time I need you to handle some business for me," Adrian stated.

"I just got back from a three hour hike. I'm cool," Corey said.

"And there's the problem. You got soft, son." Adrian smirked.

"I got smart. I have a family." Corey gritted his teeth. "Look, I don't have time for this right now. I'll take care of whatever needs to be taken care of as soon as I'm done. What is the status of my kids?"

Adrian briefly hesitated as his eyes shifted from Corey to Mia.

"What?" Mia became loud.

"Jamal says there's been a bit of a problem." Adrian pulled a cigar from his box and gently touched the delicate papers.

"Start talking," Corey said.

"Seems as if Mia's ex-husband kidnapped Melody and all the kids." Mia began to cry uncontrollably. Corey attempted to support her collapsing weight, but he felt weak himself as his heart pounded.

"But, it's under control. He doesn't have them anymore. Everyone is safe," Adrian said.

"Does Tyler know?" Corey thought of his brother-in-law.

"Yeah. He's there." Adrian nodded.

"I thought you were getting my kids?" Mia screamed at Adrian.

"Shut up and sit down," Adrian warned between the grit of his teeth.

"Don't talk to my wife like that," Corey commanded.

"I pay bills here. I will talk to whoever sets foot in this house." Adrian scowled.

Mia threw her arms in the air and started to walk away. "I'm done. I've got to go. I got to get to my kids."

Corey grabbed her arm. "No, sit down."

"Handle that, son." Adrian smirked.

"Excuse me?" Mia snatched away from him.

"I'm not letting you go. You seem to have forgotten that Andrew is after us, mostly you. Like it or not, you are safe here, for now. Let me worry about it. I will not rest until our kids are safe. Trust me." Corey gestured for his wife to sit down.

"Like I trusted you when you had me thinking you had a job," Mia quipped.

"Yeah, because regardless of what happened, the bills were paid and my family didn't go without. Because I took my vows seriously. I'm holding my end of the bargain." Corey hit his chest. "Now, are you done with trying to tear down my manhood because our kids need us and we're wasting time?"

Mia sat down and noticed the gun tucked in the Corey's pants.

"What are you doing with a gun?" Mia asked.

"What I should have done from the start. End this mess." Corey paused as he briefly looked at the sunset. "Baby, look, if I'm not back by the morning. Get on a plane. Go home. Get to our kids."

"Corey?" Mia's voice became shaky.

"Dad, I need you to get my wife home. Give her whatever she needs. Do it for me. You owe me for all the mess you put my mom through. Mia's strong and determined like my mother was even when she had to raise four kids on her own. My mother didn't deserve the hand she was dealt and neither does my wife."

"Yeah, you have my word, son." Adrian nodded.

Corey had no time for tears. Instead, he gently pulled his wife to her feet.

"You've made me a better man. You've been through some stuff that I'm not too sure many women could handle. You're my queen. I love you, Mia." Corey kissed her and walked away. He ignored her cries and pleas to stay.

Chapter Twenty-Four

He is puffed up with conceit and understands nothing. He has an unhealthy craving for controversy and for quarrels about words, which produce envy, dissension, slander, evil suspicions.
1 TIMOTHY 6:4 ESV

AN opened vodka bottle rested in the hand of Andrew. Red eyes stared straight ahead at the black and white photo of the woman in which he'd become obsessed. Women came a dime a dozen, but impressive ones were few and far between. The picture didn't do Mia justice, but it was the only thing he had to remind him of her beauty, smarts, and power to run an empire. He wanted to give her that, yet he was on the fence. She tasted power. He was sure of it. He needed more time, and she caught a conscience and ran. Mia reminded him of Peyton. When he first met the posterchild of a classic American beauty, he knew he wanted her. When he found out she was the daughter of a pastor, he needed her. Soon, Peyton became boring. She became too needy and weak. That was repulsive.

Mia had a strength that called to him like a siren of the sea. She was right when she set up shop for him to cover his money. A return had already been made on his investment based on the projections ran today. Now, she was gone. No one left Andrew, at least not alive. It didn't matter that she was married. He'd dated married women before. It didn't matter that she was with child. He could learn to be a father.

Andrew lifted the bottle to his lips and savored the heady burn of the liquid. He and the age-old drink had a relationship that extended far back to when Andrew was a child. Back then he bore the brunt of the physical and emotional abuse of his intoxicated father. Vodka could be his old man's middle name. Blinking back the old, retched memories, Andrew called for his attendant for the evening.

"Sir?" A thin man stood in the doorway. His expression was unreadable as it had been for many years. Andrew appreciated the guy's style. They had a no judgment zone.

"Jimmy, have my car pulled around front," Andrew requested.

"Okay. Will you be needing a driver?" Jimmy asked.

"No, not tonight." Andrew nodded.

"Very well. I'll give word." Jimmy turned and walked away.

Andrew pulled a lock box from under his seat and fingered the cold metal of the nine millimeter with the pads of his fingers. Slamming his fist, curses flew from him mouth. Jealousy coursed the bulging veins of his neck as he thought of what kept Mia from joining his empire—God and Corey. He couldn't compete with an imaginary being, but he could distort her vision of God by killing Corey. Death would turn her sour to the God she loved.

Picking up the gun, he could taste the spill of blood on his lips and it made him thirsty.

It was time. His car was ready. Soon, he'd be in the office of Tennessee demanding answers, and if he couldn't give them, then off with his head, too.

Andrew hopped in his car, turned on his music, and started toward the freeway. He'd be there in twenty minutes. A smile formed on his lips. As Andrew played out the death of Corey in his mind, he was oblivious to the car following him a few cars back.

Corey's eyes shifted from following Andrew's car to looking at the gun on the front passenger's seat. The screams of his children drifted through his thoughts as he imagined Edward hurting them.

Everyone relatively close to Edward knew he was going crazy, but Corey still blamed himself for what had happened.

His phone pulled him from his pity party. Looking at the caller ID, Corey almost crashed.

"Hello?" Corey answered.

"Where is my daughter?"

"Michael?" Corey looked at the phone. He wasn't sure if he should be shocked or irritated that Mia's father had called him.

"Don't make me ask you again, son." Michael's voice was deadly.

"She is with my father."

"Why aren't you with her?" Michael asked.

"Because I have to protect her and my kids."

"Is that what you're doing?" Michael asked.

"I don't think that you should have to ask that." Corey became defensive.

"A man of God doesn't have to fight with his hands, son," Michael countered.

"Michael, I don't have time for this. I'm going to have to use my hands. This has gotten far out of control and I'm not going to let anyone hurt my family."

"Like I said, this fight is not with your hands."

"Like when you beat Edward for hurting your daughter?"

"I ended up having a heart attack fighting a man who had no business with my daughter in the first place. But, let's face the truth, Edward, at the time, was no violent criminal."

"What do you mean at the time? What is he now?" Corey voice peaked. "You know what? Forget it. I gotta go."

"Turn the car around now. We can go get your wife and go home," Michael pleaded.

"How do you even know I'm driving? Wait, are you following me? How did you?" Corey shouted.

"You're family, son. I need you to be a husband to my daughter, father to your children, and the man God's called you to be," Michael shouted.

"What else am I supposed to do?" Corey looked through the rear-view mirror and noticed a blue sedan following him. It had to be Michael.

"Let's go before it's too late."

"I can't do that. My wife, my family are in danger." Corey hit the steering wheel. "Get my wife and get her out of here." Corey rambled the address of his father's house, disconnected the call, and started a conversation with God.

"What am I supposed to do? The man wants my wife. He killed Peyton. My kids are being threatened. What am I supposed to do? Tell me. Please. I know You hear me. Please. If I'm supposed to turn around, let me know. I beg of You, Father. I submit. I surrender. Help me. I am begging You. I need You. Please, Father."

Within the seconds, the noise of the city stopped. The passing bright lights of cars dimmed, and Corey felt himself alone, but safe in time that had been stopped for him. A calming peace fell over him, erasing the erratic thoughts that ran through him moments ago. He could hear the angelic words of the scripture his mother used to say play in his mind. *Submit yourselves therefore to God. Resist the devil, and he will flee from you.*

"Okay," Corey surrendered.

The busyness of the city reappeared, and he found himself stopped at a red light. Adjusting the rearview mirror, he saw Michael still behind him. Placing his eyes back on the road, he spotted Andrew with his gun cocked aiming toward him. Shots rang out and shattered the front windshield. Corey grabbed his chest and fell back against the seat.

Chapter Twenty-Five

And call upon me in the day of trouble; I will deliver you, and you shall glorify me. Psalm 50:15 ESV

Morning came quickly for Mia. Her hand touched the empty space on the bed. She desperately wished Corey was lying beside her, but he hadn't returned, and it was time for her to leave.

"Mia?" Adrian's voice invaded her thoughts.

"Yes?" Mia pulled the sheets to her chin.

Adrian leaned on the doorpost and she braced herself for bad news.

"It's time for you to go."

"Where is Corey?" Mia's voice cracked.

"I don't know. I've been calling, but no answer. There's breakfast downstairs. When you're done, I'm driving you to the airport." Adrian walked away.

Mia used the comforter to muffle her screams. "Corey, baby. I love you."

Standing to her feet, she slipped on a sundress and put her hair into a low bun at the nape of her neck. After forcing herself through the routine of brushing her teeth and washing her face, Mia threw her clothes into her suitcase along with Corey's items and padded downstairs.

She expected to see a few of Adrian's men standing around the house, but surprisingly it was empty. It was for the best. She didn't want anyone to see her distraught. When she walked into the kitchen, she was greeted with Adrian standing close to the island. His eyes narrowed and jaw clinched as he stared at something behind her.

"What?" Turning, Mia was met with a pointed gun.

Andrew smiled.

"Where's my husband?" Mia shrieked.

"Dead," Andrew said.

Mia started to leap toward Andrew, but a strong hand pulled her back and she found herself behind Adrian.

"What do you want?" Adrian asked as his eyes darted toward the window. He wondered why his guards hadn't stopped Andrew.

"What I want? No, it's who I want. I think you know who. It's that pretty lady behind you. Don't even thinking about calling your people. I took care of them." Andrew sneered.

"No, I can't do that," Adrian said.

"Okay. You're going to make this easy, but worth it. Two Phillips men dying over one woman. I can't blame you. She's special." Andrew cocked the gun.

"Why are you doing this? This is crazy. You're crazy," Mia said to Andrew.

"I… just want you to work for me." Andrew's eyebrows furrowed.

"I did. I set it up for you. What more can you want?" Mia asked.

"You. We could run this city. Hell, we could run the world," Andrew exclaimed.

"Man, this is not some twisted fairytale," Adrian shot back. "You killed my son."

"No," Mia screamed and jumped in front of Adrian.

"What are you doing?" Adrian asked Mia.

"I can't let him kill you." Mia shook her head.

Baffled, Adrian said, "You don't owe me anything."

"You're right. I don't owe you anything, but this violence has to stop." Mia started to walk toward Andrew.

"No." Adrian snatched her back. "I can't let you do this. I promised my son and I'm a man of my word."

"What? When did you grow a conscience?" Mia asked.

"Been had one. I just don't use it." Adrian peered at her then back to the gun pointed at them, "Look, I can't give you my daughter. I can't."

"I figured you wouldn't." Andrew attempted a smile and released a bullet.

The popping sound jolted Mia and Adrian gripped his arm.

"Damn," Adrian sputtered. Blood rolled down his arm.

"Look, lovely, I know you're with child. So, I don't want to traumatize you or the baby, but if you aren't over here in ten seconds, I'm going to put the next bullet in his head. And I'm pretty sure he won't be living through that."

"Andrew, look, I have a family. I would try to run each time I get. You'll get tired of chasing me," Mia pleaded.

"One." Andrew started the countdown.

"And the times I'm not running, I might be plotting to get you back for taking my husband." Mia hit her fist on the counter.

"Two."

"If you hurt my kids, there will be nothing left for me to do but kill you."

"Three."

Mia screamed and fell to her knees. "Oh my God. Help me. Help us."

"Four."

"You killed my son. You won't get away with this. I swear. I'm gonna kill you," Adrian spat.

"Oh, I would love to see that. Look, enough already. Mia get up. It's like this. God is not here to help you, but I am. God can't make you rich. I can. God didn't stop me from shooting Adrian, but I can stop myself from shooting him. Mia, you can stop me from shooting Adrian. Just get up and get over here. God can't help your children. I can." Andrew's voice rose as he gestured to himself and back to them with the gun. "I'm in charge. I'm in charge. I control my destiny and defeat. Not your God. Five."

"God, help me," Mia cried out.

"Six. I'm giving you a chance, not your God. Forget your God."

"It's going to be okay, Mia. I got so many regrets in my life. One of them is not being a better husband to my wife. I ran the streets and left my kids. Now, look at them, two dead, one in prison, and one who won't talk to me," Adrian said.

"Great speech. Hindsight is twenty-twenty. Seven."

Mia closed her eyes and pictured Corey wrapping his arms around her.

He kissed her cheek as they watched their children play in the backyard. The sun seemed to warm her body and caress her growing stomach.

"I love you." she heard Corey whisper.

"I love you, too, baby." Mia smiled.

"You are my forever." Corey touched her stomach.

"You are my forever," Mia whispered.

"Eight."

"Don't you regret your decision. Stand firm, Mia. Once you cross-over, there is no returning. I had this coming sooner or later. Let that rat shoot me." Adrian continued to hold his arm. A small pool of blood settled on the floor in which he sat. His back was against the cabinet to support his weak body.

"Eight. Get up, Mia," Andrew ordered.

"No, Andrew." Mia moved her hand to touch Adrian. Her touch startled him, but his eyes said thank you.

"I'm sorry." Adrian's eyes watered. "You're a good woman. I see everything my son sees in you. You remind me of his mother in some ways."

"Nine."

"Thank you." Mia smiled at Adrian.

"Ten." Andrew steadied the gun toward Adrian's head.

Mia's heart broke as time stood still. The whispers of her husband's promises faded along with the laughter of her children. God brought her through the last time her life had been in shambles. It was ironic to be next to the man who was ready to end her life nearly three years ago. Now they were both on the same side of a gun and praying for an immediate miracle.

"Get down. Get down. Put the gun down." Several loud voices interrupted them.

"Thank you, God!" Mia called.

"Unbelievable." Adrian shook his head in disbelief.

"What?" Andrew turned around and leered at the officers barreling into the kitchen. Guns drawn and all eyes on Andrew added tension. Andrew was itching to pull the trigger and so were the eager policeman.

"Put your gun down, Andrew," a female officer commanded. She appeared to be in charge as the others awaited her order with baited breath. "You have a few seconds left and I'll put you down."

Andrew scanned the room until his eyes came back to Mia. A look of confusion and disbelief played over his features as he was thrown to the ground. His arms were twisted into a submission hold as several officers surrounding him.

"Look at you. I guess your God heard your prayer after all. Must be some kind of woman." His face was red from being pushed into the ceramic floor. A knee jabbed him in the back causing him to grunt. Yet, he never took his eyes from her.

"Yeah, He came right on time." Mia watched the officers drag Andrew to his feet.

"I'll be out in no time. You and I are not finished." Andrew smiled.

"Shut up. We got you on two attempts of murder. You won't be seeing her unless she comes to visit you in the pen," the arresting officer shouted.

"We'll see about that. You don't know who I am, but you'll find out," Andrew threatened as he was pulled to his feet, escorted from the house, and read his rights.

"Adrian Phillips, you have the right to remain silent. Anything you say can and will be used against you in a court of law. You have the right to an attorney. If you cannot afford an attorney, one will be provided for you. Do you understand the rights I have just read to you?"

"Yeah." Adrian took a deep breath. "What are my charges?"

"In a nutshell, possession, manufacturing, and distribution," the female officer responded. "You've been shot. I need a medic. With these rights in mind, do you wish to speak to me?"

"Yeah." Adrian's head dropped.

"I need to see my son. I need to identify my son," Adrian said.

"What do you mean? Identify?" the officer asked.

"My husband. Corey Phillips. He's...he's...dead. Andrew killed him." Another wave of pain coursed through Mia as her voice shook.

"No, Corey Phillips was being held with the criminal threat, but that looks like it won't hold. He was released hours ago."

"What? Where is he?" Mia cried.

"My son. My son is alive?" Adrian whispered.

"Mrs. Phillips, I'll need to talk with you. Can we go to the station?" the female officer asked.

"Am I being arrested?" Once again, Mia's life flashed before her eyes.

"Did you commit a crime?" the officer asked.

Mia did not respond.

"She didn't do anything. Everything is my fault. You have my word," Adrian spoke.

"Hmmm, we'll see. My name is Agent Melanie Stevens. This way, Mia." The officer guided Mia toward the front door.

"Secure the suspect. I want around the clock surveillance on him. Let me know the minute he is released into our custody," Melanie spoke to her unit before exiting he house with Mia.

Chapter Twenty-Six

But seek first the kingdom of God and his righteousness and all these things will be added to you. Therefore do not be anxious about tomorrow, for tomorrow will be anxious for itself. Sufficient for the day is its own trouble. MATTHEW 6:33-34

COREY sat on the woody pier and watched the waters of the Pacific Ocean. His eyes fixated on the horizon. God has spared his life. The police thought it was a freak of nature that Andrew shot through the front windshield and missed Corey completely. The bullets that entered the car were reported as bent and no one could understand nor identify the reason why they had all missed Corey. Glass had been shattered. The debris alone should have at least caused a scratch, but there was nothing. The paramedics at the scene has even cut off his shirt as he lay unconscious in the car searching and prodding for a hole or bruise. Corey tried to remember what happened, but his recollection of the event was at best vague. He called out to God on his way to kill a man. He stopped at the light and Andrew walked up to the front of his car and unleashed a hail of bullets. Everything went dark. He'd been told that he possibly had fainted from shock.

The splashing of the water on the large rocks below was rhythmic and provided a peace as thoughts of his family passed through his mind. He and Mia's relationship had been tumulus from the start.

From him leaving her high and dry for ten years, to him returning and whisking her away to commit a crime in L.A., then back again to deal with the violent Andrew. On top of it, he was still jobless and broke. There was no way he'd been the best husband or father to his children. Edward had kidnapped his children. Even the idea of all the mayhem made Corey feel defeated. Their lives had been straight out of some criminal action adventure film and for that he was ashamed. Forget about being a living testimony. He was a walking nightmare. Mia and his children deserved better. He had to leave in order to make them safe.

"This is a hell of a story, Mrs. Phillips." Melanie sat back in her chair and watched Mia.

"It is, but it is the truth." A sense of relief washed over Mia. She hadn't told the entire story to anyone, not even Corey. She assumed he already knew since he experienced the situation with her.

"I've been trying to put Andrew behind bars for a while. He's... well, let's just say the streets are safer without people like him on them." Melanie eyes shifted to a picture behind Mia. Mia turned her eyes toward the photo. A tall brunette sat smiling while hugging a younger Melanie.

"Seems like a personal connection," Mia said.

"Something like that. Long story, but your story is more intriguing." Melanie changed the subject.

"I don't know. I just know that I'm glad it's over. At least, I think it's over." Mia still wondered if she would be arrested.

"Here's the deal. Money laundering is a felony, but it seems as if you acted under duress and forced pretenses. I can more than likely get this thrown out. You've given us two big fish, Adrian and Andrew, but I need your signed word that you will be willing to testify when the time comes."

Mia thought of her father-in-law. She hoped she would not have to see him during his trial. "Will I have to testify against Adrian?"

"Yes," Melanie admitted.

"Yes, I'll do it," Mia answered.

Melanie pushed documents in front of Mia to sign.

Taking a deep breath, Mia signed them. "Am I free to go?"

"Sure. Go home." Melanie smiled.

Mia stood. She was unsure of where to go. At this point she didn't want any of her clothes at Adrian's home. She needed to see her husband and children. That was all that mattered.

"One more thing," Melanie said.

"Yeah?"

"What's up with you and this God thing? I mean, I'm not sure if I believe or not, but you speak of Him as if He's the best thing that has ever happened to you." Melanie glanced at the picture of the young woman and then back to Mia.

"I'll tell you what, He's never left me. He's never let me down." Mia smiled.

"And where might I find Him? How do I even know He values me?" Melanie was sincere.

Mia pulled a sticky note and pen from Melanie's desk and wrote, "Start here." Mia put the paper on her desk.

"Matthew 6:26-34?" Melanie questioned.

"Yes, Agent Stevens. Start there. Thank you for all that you've done."

Melanie nodded and pulled a small bible from her desk. Mia closed the door.

Surprise is what Mia felt as she exited the station and saw her father standing at the foot of the steps. His peaceful expression made her feel safe. Although she longed for the touch of her husband, she felt security in the arms of her father. The familiarity of his embrace brought back the memories of childhood.

"Daddy," Mia cried as she rested her head on his chest.

"Baby girl." He squeezed her.

"I love you."

"I love you, too, Mia."

"How did you know I was here?"

"I'm your father, I'm supposed to know."

"Would you happen to know if my children are safe and where my husband is?" Mia asked. She pulled her head back to look at her father.

"The children are with Mom, and Corey… He'll meet us back in Indy." Michael forced a smile.

"What? Why?" Mia tried not to get angry, but disappointment and hurt were getting the best of her.

"He needs some time to think. This has been a lot," Michael said.

"Yeah, I would think so. I…can't right now. Why would he just leave me here like this? I'm his wife. We've been through too much."

Michael said nothing as he allowed his daughter to vent. A few people did double takes as Mia let loose.

It's time to go home. How's Melody?" Mia changed the subject.

"Long story. She'll be fine."

"Our plane leaves this evening. You need to get your things." Michael held her hand and started to walk toward the parking lot.

"There is nothing left for me here. I want nothing to do with any clothing I have here. It would bring back awful memories. And I sure don't want to go back to Adrian's house. I'm fine." Mia lightly squeezed her father's hand.

"Okay. Well, let's go. We can grab something to eat. We gotta feed my newest grandson." Michael winked.

"Really, Dad? It could be a girl." Mia smiled.

"Hmmm." Michael nodded. "We'll see."

As they got in the car, Mia slid her phone from her purse. She was desperately hoping for a notification from Corey. There was nothing, not as much as a wave from her social media messages. Wrapping her head around Corey's dismissal of her wasn't working. Typing a message would help her release the hurt.

Well, I'm glad to know that you're okay. I thought you were dead and my world ended. Just leaving the police station. Wishing you were here. Why aren't you talking to me, babe?

Moments later…

I love you, Mia. I'll see you soon.

Mia relaxed her head against the seat and closed her eyes. Corey's brief response did ease some of her pain.

"Baby girl, get some rest. GPS says we have a thirty -minute drive to the restaurant." Michael patted his daughter's hand.

"Okay." Mia smiled.

Chapter Twenty-Seven

He who finds a wife finds a good thing and obtains favor from the Lord. Proverbs 18:22 ESV

MELODY sat in her living room watching reruns of a once popular sitcom from her childhood. All the parts of the show that were knee slapping funny failed to produce any response from her. Instead, she watched the show and tried to push the tears back in her eyes. She would get over her miscarriage. That was certain, but what she couldn't manage is Tyler's persistence in nailing Andrew to a wall that he neglected their vows. If they hadn't been trapezing around L.A. none of this would have happened. They would be adding another beautiful baby to their family. That's all she wanted was a family. Perhaps, Tyler was not the one.

A jingle of keys let her know that Tyler was home. Well, he'd been home. He'd been staying in his parents' house since she was released from the hospital. She asked him to leave her be and he did his best to honor her request, but every few hours like clockwork, he'd come in to check the air, pour her something to drink, or bring her food. The sadness and regret in his eyes was enough to make her weak, but her bitterness fought to remain a while longer to remind them both of what had transpired.

"Hey, baby." Tyler carefully approached his wife.

Swollen eyes watched her and she quickly looked away.

"You don't have to talk, but I want you to listen."

Melody merely nodded

"I messed up, Melody. I disregarded you, us, in the process in trying to punish someone. It hurts to know my sister died by the hands of him, but I know now that she died because of her choices. It's not my fault. It's definitely not your fault. I blamed the very woman that God gave me for something that had nothing to do with her. I need you in my life, Melody. I need Lena. I need us to be a family. And if it takes me forever, then I'll apologize to you every day. I've been a hypocrite. I've been telling the people to trust God to fight their battles, but I did not." Tyler slumped in his seat as his head fell in his hands.

"We lost a child, Tyler."

"Yes, we did."

"You knew I wanted a baby. I didn't even know I was pregnant." Melody bit her quivering lip.

"I know. I… You can still be a mother to our child. We have one beautiful one already. She needs us, Melody."

"Yeah." Melody nodded, "I know."

"Can we start over? Please. Give us a chance. You know that we're meant to be together. The moment I laid eyes on you, I knew that you were my wife. I prayed for my queen and the moment I saw you with Peyton that night, I knew God had answered my prayers. I just hadn't expected Him to answer so soon."

Closing her eyes, Melody remembered. When she saw him that evening, her fluttering heart and immediate connection signaled a future that she had wished for so long. She stole it from her sister with the wrong man, but she had been given redemption. God had sent her Tyler.

"Okay," Melody whispered.

"Okay?" Tyler moved closer.

"Okay to us. I love you."

Heaviness removed itself from Tyler's chest and he nearly leapt from his seat to rest his head on the lap of his wife.

"The moment that you're ready, we'll start on our family." Tyler pulled back to reach his wife. He wrapped his arms around her waist while pulling her into his embrace. Taking in a deep breath, the familiar scent of lavender touched his nose.

"I do." Tyler blinked.

"I do what?" Lips parted, Melody waited.

"I do want to be with you for the rest of our lives. I do want you to know that you were made for me and I for you. I do want you to know that I will be the best husband that I can be." Pulling his face to meet Melody's lips, they sealed the promise with a kiss.

A knock on the door interrupted their bliss.

"Come in," Tyler called with eyes still on his wife.

"Sorry to interrupt." Charles' eyes traveled between the both of them. Dropping his shoulders, the anticipated tension left and a smile lit up his face. "I see you too are talking. Thank God."

"Yes, we are," Tyler responded.

"Brandy and your mom are taking Lena to the park." Charles sat.

"They're what?" Curiosity widened Melody's eyes.

"Yes, wow, right?" Lips twitched with a smile as Charles nodded his head.

"You mean Amelia is up and walking around?" Melody asked.

"Yes, without much medication. It's a miracle. Brandy has been such a blessing to us. Amelia says it's like old times," Charles said.

"Well, does this mean Brandy will be here for a while?" Tyler asked.

"Yes, she says she can be here as long as she is needed."

"The weather seems nice for a day at the park. Let me check the news." Melody reached for the television remote.

"No dear. Not right now." Charles shifted his eyes to his son then back to Melody.

"What? What is going on?" Melody questioned.

"We're all over the news?" Tyler said.

"Okay. Why?" Melody asked.

"Edward has been arrested for murder. It doesn't look good. State wants to charge him with first degree," Charles said.

"What?" Melody's voice cracked. "He killed someone? Who?"

"A young man who worked at the hospital. He had a wife and kid." Tyler touched his wife's hand.

"I can't believe this. They connected him to us?" Melody questioned.

"Yes, of course the old story of you, Mia, and Edward is being highlighted again. It will pass, baby. I promise. Our lawyers and PR agent is all over it. We will be issuing a statement soon," Tyler said.

"When?" Melody asked.

"We need you to look over it," Charles added.

"He tried to kill me, too." Remembering her ex-lover's chokehold, her hand touched her throat.

"What? You never told me this. When?" Tyler stood and paced the room.

"At my sister's house, when he brought Lena and I there. I remember him hitting me. Knocking me to the ground and choking me. Soon after, my stomach began to cramp."

"Why didn't you tell me this?" The loudness of Tyler's voice startled her.

"Wouldn't have changed anything. You were in L.A.," Melody said.

"I mean afterwards," Tyler said.

"Like I said, wouldn't have changed anything." Melody turned her head to look out the window.

Silence carried throughout the room. Revelation had reared its head and blame came back to that of Tyler. Perhaps things could have been different if he'd been present.

"I need some air." Tyler walked out.

"Tyler," Melody called.

"Give him some time. This is such a tragedy." Charles shook his head.

Chapter Twenty-Eight

So that the tested genuineness of your faith—more precious than gold that perishes though it is tested by fire—may be found to result in praise and glory and honor at the revelation of Jesus Christ. 1 Peter 1:7 ESV

A duffle bag sat on the bed and Corey filled it with a few of his items. An uncomfortable silence carried throughout the house since they'd been back home. Knowing that his family was safe made Corey grateful, but still he felt responsible for putting his wife and children through unnecessary harm. Had he taken a leap of faith and told Tennessee no the moment he asked for them to go to L.A., his family would not have had to endure such terror. So, this all came back to his faith. Where had it been? He didn't even have enough faith when he came to being truthful on his resume.

"What are you doing?" Mia entered the room with CJ on her hip. The baby rubbed his eyes and stared at his father. A gummy smile appeared on his face.

"What does it look like?" Corey spoke softly. Regret instantly ran through him. It wasn't his intention to be harsh, but self loathe regulated him.

"I don't deserve that," Mia said as she walked toward the bed and glanced in the bag.

"I need to go." Corey placed a few shirts in the bag.

"And do what?" Mia put CJ on the floor and closed the door. Instantly the infant crawled toward his father.

"You're right. You don't deserve this. You don't need me around here broke or keeping some minimum wage job to only be able to pay the light bill every month. I'm not used to this. I used to make thousands of dollars a day and now I'm pinching pennies. I got you up here committing crimes. I'm good, Mia. You don't need this." Corey choked through his words.

"We've been home for a week in this uncomfortable quiet, faking like everything is okay." Mia threw her arms in the air. "You know what? The moment I took my vows, I said for better or worse. This is our worse. I mean it was our worse. Did you think for one moment that when we were in this mess the first time, that I was going to sacrifice my life and salvation to live a life of crime with you. I love you, but that was not an option. That's what marriage is about. That is what commitment looks like," Mia said.

"I don't know." Corey picked up CJ who was trying to eat the carpet.

"You know what? If you leave, don't come back. I'm so tired of quitters. I've already been down heartbreak road. I'm used to it. So, get your stuff and go." Mia wiped her eyes.

"It's like that?" Corey watched his wife.

"You chose to leave, not me. You know, Agent Stevens told me that they can't understand how the bullets from Andrew's gun did not hit your body. From where he was standing, it was a sure shot. Almost like point blank range, Corey. They even have video footage from the traffic light camera of him getting out the car, standing in front of the car, and letting loose three bullets. Not even one hit you. If you don't see the Hand of God on your life, then, maybe you should walk out," Mia said.

"Mia?" Corey nearly whispered.

"I can't afford to stop my life again. I have two kids and one on the way. I have to survive for them. I love you with all I have, but there are three people depending on me. I don't have a choice but to keep going. So, if you want to run, then run, but that's not what a man whose life was saved should be doing. God didn't stop the bullet for you to run. He stopped it for you to prevail." Mia started to walk away.

"Where are you going?" Corey asked.

"Does it even matter?" Mia closed the door behind her.

Baymont Mental Hospital held mental patients including ones who committed criminal offenses. Edward had been involuntarily admitted here for close to a week under observation and medication. Nearly every news media outlet had run the story of Edward, the ex-lover of Melody Deen. The past seemed to once again rear its ugly head and use its face to distract from the promises of the future.

Mia walked down the crisp, white hall of the facility to the receptionist. The straight faces of the medical staff said no nonsense. Armed security was in nearby stations to ensure safety. A few even nodded their heads her way. She nodded back.

"Excuse me." Mia stopped at the rounded desk and looked at the middle-aged blonde woman peering at a computer screen.

"One moment." The woman never looked up. The tapping of the keyboard was almost the only noise in the quiet room.

Mia wondered if the woman was always nonchalant. At most hospitals she visited, everyone was so polite. She remembered that this was no ordinary hospital. She wasn't visiting a sick relative. Well, perhaps she was according to reports. Edward was mentally ill.

"I'm here to see Edward Johnson." Mia knew she was taking a chance by coming here, but she had to try.

"Are you a relative?" Blue eyes scanned her.

"I'm the mother of his child," Mia responded.

"Wife?"

"Ex-wife."

"That's even trickier. I'll call, but I'm sure this visit will not happen."

"I'll wait while you call."

A breathy sigh escaped the woman's mouth as she made the call. Mia didn't care. A man who she has once promised herself, slept with, cried with, and raised a child was somewhere in this facility. She needed to know what he'd been thinking. Melody wasn't providing much information and neither was Tyler. When she asked, their response had consistently been not to worry. A chapter that was once closed had been violently reopened for the world to see. She was glad the headlines spoke of Melody being the ex-lover of a madman and not the tragic affair that propelled her into a life of crime. Taylor didn't have much to say either. She stayed with her grandparents for the past week and insisted on checking on CJ on a daily basis.

"Ma'am, please take the elevator to the fifth floor. Someone will meet you there."

"Does this mean that I get to see him?" Mia was hopeful.

"I'm not sure. Good luck." She pointed toward the elevator.

The elevator ride was quick. When the door opened, two officers greeted her along with an unpleasant medicinal smell. The stern faces of the guards mirrored the ones downstairs.

"Ma'am, we've been asked to take you to the meeting room. Please follow me."

Mia followed the tall man to a small waiting room and was soon greeted by a small man in a tweed suit.

"Hello, Mrs. Phillips. My name is John Petters. I am Edward's psychiatrist." The man smiled, revealing small, white teeth.

"Hello." Mia shook the hand that was offered to her.

"So, you're here to see Edward. I must say. I'm surprised you're here." Dr. Petters scrunched his lips.

"I need to see him." Mia hoped the man would be understanding. She didn't want trouble. She just wanted closure.

"It would be against every good judgment that I have to allow you to see him. Edward committed a crime of passion in order to get to you. He is under the impression that you both will someday get back together. And we both know that is not a possibility, but in his obscured mind, that is a strong chance." Dr. Petters peered at Mia.

"You're right, but I can tell him that. Let me get a chance to let him know. From what I gather, meds and therapy haven't worked. I am raising our daughter. I need something, Doctor. I need something to go back and tell her. She's been through too much." Mia tried to remain calm, but her lingering thoughts of Taylor made her weak. Taylor's biological mother had become victim to the fast life years ago. The last she'd heard of the woman, she was the girlfriend of an up and coming rapper in Miami. Mia had even seen her in a few social media posting with the artist. Now her biological father was more than likely going to do time for murder. Taylor could barely function knowing that she could have killed her own father while trying to protect her aunt.

"I could lose my job." Dr. Petters seemed to be considering Mia's plea.

"Or you could make your job a lot easier. Our daughter needs answers. She needs something from her father. I know Edward can't be in a strait jacket banging his head against the wall. That's not the man I know," Mia said.

"He could very well be in a strait jacket after this." Dr. Petters shook his head.

"Would it change his circumstance? I don't think so," Mia pressed.

"I'm giving you a supervised five minutes behind glass. No word of this to the media." Dr. Petters touched Mia's arm as they both stood.

"You have my word." Mia nodded.

Getting to Edward was not as simple as Mia thought. Walking through a series of hallways and doors, Mia knew she would need an escort back to the first-floor receptionist. The checkered pattern floors and white walls were continuous. The caged windows reminded her of an insane asylum out of a horror film. The reality that her ex-husband was in this place indefinitely caused immediate grief. She once was in love with this man. They shared a beautiful daughter who would more likely never see him again. Four years ago, they were planning to get pregnant and sell their home to move to a new housing development in the city of Avon a few miles outside of Indianapolis. Now she was remarried with two children by her childhood love. One man was killing to be with her and another was questioning whether or not he was good enough to stay.

Finally, they arrived. One room was separated by large glass that reached the ceiling. Armed guards were on the side that Mia was sure Edward would soon be entering. Sitting down in a chair, Mia watched as Dr. Petters used a code to enter the other side of the room. He briefly spoke with one of the stoic looking guards and they both disappeared behind another door.

Sighing, Mia imagined being single. It was hard to think of the possibility, but her husband was at home considering what they'd fought to keep. He did have a point; a lot of drama and chaos transpired, and the more Mia thought of it, heavy turmoil had worn out its welcome. She'd experienced more than many and defeat was a breath from leaving her lips, but a drive kept her pushing and focusing on yet another test of faith.

A buzz snatched her from her thoughts and she watched her ex knight in shining armor be escorted to the seat directly in front of her. His unkempt appearance was saddening. Edward's eyes focused on her as he made small steps with shackles on his ankle. The same chains that were on his ankles were attached to his wrists reminding Mia of a wild animal being domesticated. Dr. Petters was close to Edward, almost waiting for him to have a meltdown.

Thinking about what she had seen in the movies, Mia picked up the phone and Edward soon followed.

"Hey," Mia said

Edward hesitated before speaking as he scanned her face. "Hey."

Mia's free hand automatically touched the glass.

"I've done something beyond repair," Edward said.

"I know," Mia whispered.

"Looks like this place will be my home." Edward's eyes shifted from the ceiling to the floor, then back to Mia.

"I don't know." Mia was honest.

"I k..k…illed a man." Edward's voice cracked and unchecked tears streamed down his face.

Mia nodded her head and willed the painful lump in her throat away. "Yeah, you did. Why? Why did you do this?"

Edward's fist hit the table causing Dr. Petters to quickly lean forward and give a warning look to Mia. Edward spoke, "I was trying to get to you. I thought we had a chance…like it used to be."

"Edward, we had our time and then the unthinkable happened. I have forgiven you, but I also moved on. I will always love you, but I am not coming back to you." Mia fought back tears.

"I…it hurts, but I think I know. Something tells me that I messed up and for that I'm sorry. Somehow, I have got to let you go. Taylor? Tell Taylor that I love her. She's in good hands. At least I know that a part of me will forever be connected to you. Thank you for taking care of my daughter, being her mother. When you look at her, don't see me. See you. She's everything that represents you. Beauty. Strength. Kindness. Love. I'm sorry for this, Mia." Edward stood.

"Thank you for this." Mia wiped her eyes.

"My meds are working. It doesn't hurt me as much to see you walk away." Edward made a poor attempt to make light of what probably would be their final goodbye.

"I won't forget you. Taylor does have the good parts of you. She's resilient. She's clever. She's witty." Mia stood, too.

"Goodbye, Mia. Corey's a lucky man. Tell Melody I'm sorry and that Lena has the best mother that she could possibly get. Take care." Edward touched the glass. Then, he turned and walked away.

Mia watched him shuffle away the same way he entered the room. He did not look back.

Twenty-Nine

The blessing of the Lord makes rich, and he adds no sorrow with it. PROVERBS 10:22 ESV

COREY watched CJ sleep. The miniature replica slept peacefully in his crib. They played for most of the day and now it was close to 10:00 p.m. Mia was still not home and loneliness crept in him. Knowing he'd hurt his wife was unbearable. It hadn't been his intention. Now, all he wanted was for her to come home. Calling her parents was out of the question for now. He didn't want to be the source of their stress once again.

The deep need to see his wife outweighed his thoughts on leaving his family. He could not leave what God had given. Yet, being unemployed and watching his stressed wife try to take care of the family was sickening. Corey wanted her to have a choice in staying home to provide security and fragrance to their home.

Closing CJ's door, Corey made his way to the living room. A long sigh escaped his lips and he closed his eyes. Calling his wife would be pointless. It was obvious she needed time. He'd caused this. Had he not been wrapped in his feelings, they could be holding each other right now as they usually did when CJ took naps.

"God, help me," Corey called out. "Thank You, Father, for giving me life. Thank You for bringing my family safely home. My life has been far from perfect, but I'm asking for restoration. I'm nothing without You. Have mercy on me, God, as You've done countless times before. Forgive me. Cover my marriage, God. Protect us from this world that is trying to tear us away from You. Give me a way to provide for my family. I ask this is Jesus' name. Amen."

There was nothing left to do now but be patient. A peace dropped over Corey as he stood and walked into the kitchen. A pile of mail sat on the counter. Neither he nor Mia had opened a single piece of mail since they'd been back. Just by eyeing it, he could tell most of it was junk except for a few bills. A large envelope peeked through the ads and coupons. Reading it, Corey saw that the letter was to him from his former employer that had let him go. Curious fingers tore open the envelope and removed the letter.

Dear Mr. Corey Phillips,

Baker, Jones, & Smith Financial is a company founded on the pillars of hard work and integrity. We support young professionals looking to add to this financial institution that has been ranked in the Forbes 500 companies for the past fifteen years. Our goal is to provide professional and highly effective advice to clients that have contracted us to provide financial plans that work and turn profit.

The board has made a decision about your employment with the firm. After investigation we've determined...

Corey heard the front door unlock and quickly folded the letter, placing it on the table. His wife was home. He didn't have time to focus on a letter that held the fate of his job. Walking into the living room, he watched her.

Her soft, deep brown hair was braided in a single plait down her back. Smooth skin glowed in her purple sundress that gently caressed her curves. Lips were lightly parted as if she wanted to say hello, but instead her searching eyes sought answers. He was ready to give an answer as his eyes rested on her slightly rounded belly. Pride puffed his chest as he realized this queen held yet another one of his children. His wife carried his name and his wife carried a legacy that would forever be tied to them.

"I love you." Corey walked to her and pulled her in his arms. "I'm sorry. I can't leave you. Forgive me for even one moment thinking that leaving was the best answer. I want what's best for us."

The familiar soft scent of lavender touched his nose and provided solace to him. He felt her soft weight find comfort in his arms.

"I love you, too." Mia looked up and scanned Corey's face.

The curve of her neck called for his fingers to touch. The angles of her cheeks called for him to caress. Her parted lips called for him to kiss. Soft lavender danced in his flared nostrils one more time before he submitted to the call of the siren. Spending tender moments enraptured in what had been created for him heightened his senses. This was where his heart was. This was home.

"Corey?" Mia broke the kiss and fanned herself.

"Baby?" Corey was not ready for their intimacy to end.

"You, uh, um got me weak." Mia blushed.

"That's how you have me every day," Corey said.

"Hmm." Mia smiled. "I need some water." She walked toward the kitchen.

"Yeah, well, we are finishing this later on today." Corey admired his wife as she walked away.

"We better." Mia blew him a kiss over her shoulder.

"Don't tempt me to make it now, girl." Corey laughed.

"Look at all this mail." Mia picked up a handful of envelopes.

"One of them is from Baker, Jones, and Smith." Corey pointed to the folded paper.

"Did you read it?" Mia picked it up.

"Started it but didn't finish it." Corey gave a half smile.

"Good or bad news?" Mia asked.

"Baby, I don't know." Corey sighed.

"You want me to read it?" Mia asked.

"Yeah. Drop down to the second paragraph," Corey said.

"Okay." Mia started to read.

The board has made a decision about your employment with the firm. After investigation we've determined that your actions in omitting information from your resume and application do not reflect company expectations and policy. However, since your employment date, you have increased our profit margins, contracted several new high-profile clients, and maintained professionalism at all time. Your absence of thirty days to date has served as your paid and unpaid suspension. Your return date is Monday, July...

"Baby!" Mia stopped reading. "You got your job back."

"What?" Corey pulled the letter from Mia's hand.

"We have got to celebrate." Mia threw her arms in the air and hopped around the kitchen.

"We do." Corey laughed, watching his wife attempt to dance.

"Let's go get Taylor and get some ice cream," Mia suggested.

"Alright, baby."

"I'm going to go get CJ." Mia started for the stairs.

Corey looked up. "Thank You, God. You are so good. I love You, forever."

Chapter Thirty

MELODY didn't have enough courage to sit in the sanctuary to hear her husband minister the Word. Everything seemed to be spinning in and out of control. She was once again the center of attention with Edward going crazy and ending a man's life. It was sickening and saddening at the same time that their daughter would grow up to one day know that her biological father killed someone. Embarrassment also showed its ugly head to bring up her past. The sting of her actions did not bother her as much as it had before. Most people in the church knew her story and admired her courage to admit her sin and journey of repentance. She'd even shared her story to encourage others that continually God extends grace and mercy to the lives of sinners.

Perhaps it was just today, that she didn't feel like being a part of the people's scrutiny. She didn't want another people's choice and opinion trial. No public verdict was welcome especially if it was one that might hurt her daughter.

Watching from the office monitor, Melody could see that praise and worship was nearly over. Normally, she and Tyler would enter during the last part of the singing. Yet she watched him enter alone. Perhaps it was best. They hadn't talked much since he had yet another epiphany about him leaving his family to pursue Peyton's killer. In the end, Andrew was arrested, but not by any doing of Tyler.

"Darling, are you going into service?" Amelia Deen walked into the room.

Melody smiled. Her mother-in-law reminded her of the first time they met. The regal matron wore a flowing floral maxi dress trimmed in gold bands that gave hint to royalty. The hair Melody had once cut had grown out. The golden tresses were now past her shoulders. However, she wore her hair in a bun at the nape of her neck. A few wispy tendrils touched her face. Gone was the hardness and what replaced it was something very close to freedom. Brandy's extended visit was doing wonders.

"I don't know, Amelia." Melody's eyes rested on the monitor. Tyler was now seated. His face appeared stern. "It's good to see you at church today."

"I figured that I had to stop faking crazy one of these days. I can't play hooky from church forever." Amelia tried to make a joke.

"Amelia." Melody sighed at her mother-in-law's poor attempt to be funny.

"I'm trying to lighten you up."

"I know. I'm just exhausted. This whole ordeal has made me just want to quit, pack it up, and forget it all."

"Even Tyler?"

"No. What I mean is to just…just…"

"Just take a break from being in the church limelight because everybody is judging you and has an opinion even when you're trying to figure it out yourself." Amelia gave a half smile.

"Pretty much."

"Oh, well if I was to even consider what people thought of me when I had my meltdown. I mean, what they partly may have said was right and I didn't want to face it. I could have been a better mother to Peyton, but I couldn't have stopped what happened to her. I know that. What kept me in bed mostly was the thoughts of the people. It was enough already to deal with my own mistakes, but I just didn't want to see it on the faces of so many," Amelia said.

"But, it's not me this time feeling like that. It's Tyler," Melody said.

"Yes, but Tyler is out there and you're in here. He is upset that he let you down. It's a hard pill to swallow, but he needs you by his side. You in here only reinforces the fact that he left you and possibly put you in harm's way. That's a horrible feeling. Remember, I know firsthand." Amelia touched Melody's shoulder.

"Yes. Amelia, we lost a child." Melody's voice cracked.

"I lost a daughter and my son lost a sister, but somehow we found a will to live," Amelia said.

"You want me to forget?" Melody pulled away from Amelia's hand to face her. Brown eyes met blue ones.

"I want you to live."

Melody closed her eyes. "I do want to live."

"Then get up and let Tyler see that he still has purpose with you."

"He should know that, Amelia," Melody said

"And God knows He created you, but there's nothing like a good praise." Amelia patted Melody's hand.

Melody smiled. "Okay."

"See you soon." Amelia walked away.

"Well, here I go."

Tyler sat in the pulpit and listened. The great Charles Deen had the microphone and he was having a full gospel explosion on stage. The church was in an uproar. Tyler wondered if the crowd stood on their dancing feet partly because they were happy to see the pastor that they had once knew. The old Charles Deen, the pre-Peyton's death, Charles Deen boldly held the mic. Yet, Tyler sat still and closed his eyes while being caught between hoping his stoic response to his father would go unnoticed and not giving a care who saw him sit there.

He thought of Melody and how he'd ultimately let her down. Edward's vicious attack had a lot to do with Melody's miscarriage, but Tyler felt it was his own neglect to the marriage that ended their innocent child's life. He wondered if the life that ended way too soon was a girl or boy. He envisioned watching his wife give birth to a beautiful baby. If it had been a girl, he would have considered naming her Peyton.

Melody was somewhere in the church watching from afar. He knew she was too weak to come out here. He didn't blame here. She was done with scandal. She'd left Indianapolis to avoid scandal and humiliation and now she was hit with a metal baseball bat full of déjà vu. They needed more time. They needed something fresh and the opportunity that his father had proposed to him this morning was something he was willing to consider. Actually, he already said yes and prayed his wife wouldn't throw a fit in making a decision without consulting her. Right now, if she refused, he'd honor her wishes, but he was praying that his discernment was telling him that she wanted and needed this

Tyler's thoughts shifted back to the church. People were settling, and his father was winding down. He was hoping that perhaps his father would continue service and give the message, but that was not so. Charles Deen was adamant that his son have a word today.

Tyler walked coolly to the podium and looked at the faces in the audience. Many were familiar and others not so. However, he knew that they all shared a commonality. That was they knew the Deen story and many of them wanted to know more.

"Praise God." Tyler spoke into the microphone and touched his bible.

"Hallelujah," hundreds responded.

"I don't know about you, but I came to give God praise in the place. He's been good to me!" Tyler started and he did feel that way regardless of his circumstance. Actually, he could shout thinking that he could be dead or in jail trying to bring justice to his sister.

"I come to you today to give a Word, but before I do, I need to talk to you. Can I share part of my heart with you, Green Pastures?" Tyler waited for the congregation.

"Yes," voices responded.

"Good, because today, I have to speak. I have to share. I have to let you in a part of my life so that God may get the glory. Please understand that this is not meant to entertain, but give you an idea of a man who lost hope in God... A man who almost lost his wife." Tyler watched the people. A few covered their hearts and others released small gasps. It was now or never.

"Of course you know that over a year ago, my sister, Peyton, was found murdered in Los Angeles. My beautiful, dear sister who if I could turn back the hands of time, I would beg her not to go, no, I would forbid her from going to California had I known the outcome of her fate. Pictures play in my mind of how she took her last breath and let me tell you, it gives me nightmares to imagine her there on the ground. Bullets in her chest, labored breathing, lying there with regrets. Was she scared? Did she say, 'God, help me. Help me, Dad. Help me, Momma, Help me, Tyler.'? A life of perpetual sin took her there. The spirit of anger, bitterness, and loneliness tore at her like a legion of diseases. Yet, I still blamed myself for not being her knight in shining armour to rescue her from all the things that tore at her heart and separated her from God. I blamed myself."

Green Pastured waited as Tyler swallowed and willed away a weep that fought to escape his mouth. His fight caused both women and men to dab at the corners of their eyes. Perhaps they remembered the fight. Everyone had experienced the fight. The fight to hold on to a loved one that had succumbed to the world. Memories of a fight that once had them clawing for redemption on a rope laden with oil.

Tyler continued, "So, I did what I thought was right and I let my flesh scream revenge. I wanted to find the person who so recklessly, so carelessly, took my sister's life. I wanted him to feel what she felt. I wanted to squeeze the life from him. I refused to recognize that this… this… person was also a child of God. Romans 12:19 say, dearly beloved, avenge not yourselves, but rather give place unto wrath, for it is written, vengeance is mine; I will repay, saith the Lord."

Amelia quietly cried from the pulpit and Charles stood in honor and support. His eyes, too, screamed for the release of tears, but he did not surrender. He only nodded and closed his eyes every now and then. If one looked closely, Charles Deen's lips would move in prayer.

"I didn't listen. Truth is, I didn't believe God would work for me this time. I believed God for the issues of others, but my faith was not strong enough to cover me. My faith was gone. Behind this smile was a man screaming and drowning in a pool of bitterness. My determination took my attention away from what God had gifted me. God created a woman for me and I placed a living, breathing, gift from God in the corner to pursue something that was already dead. And right then and there, the devil had me where he wanted me. I built a foundation with cracks. My foundation to avenge my sister was wayward. My distance from my wife allowed the enemy to steal, to kill, and to destroy. But yet right now I stand vindicated by God's grace. I am vindicated by His mercy. I am vindicated because of His favor. I thank God for the scales of anger to be removed from my eyes. My wife was nearly killed in my pursuit. In a flash, of me calling on God to be released by the hands of my own spiritual death, I felt freed. I returned home. To my wife, I publicly apologize for my sins against God and my neglect toward you. I apologize to our daughter, Lena. Daddy will always be your protector and although you may not be my biological daughter, we are connected by the spirit and that connection is stronger than blood."

"We love you, Pastor!" a woman hollered from the congregation.

"We support you, Pastor! Make it plain! Amen!" a man followed in support.

"My father brought some news to me this morning about our campus in Pennsylvania. We put it on hold for a while after Peyton's death. But, it's ready. There is life. There is life. There is life. I was asked to take over officially as senior pastor in thirty days, but I will not go unless my wife is willing. I haven't brought it to her yet. I probably shouldn't have said anything yet, but..." Tyler smiled. A bit of nervousness touched him as he wondered if mentioning the Pennsylvania opportunity was abrupt. "We'll find..." Tyler stopped.

A quiet came over the bustling church. Air stood still and suspense held its breath as Melody quietly entered the back of the sanctuary. Tyler watched his wife and remembered the first time he saw her. Her beauty captivated him then and mesmerized him now. Her regal stature and soft, feminine curves screamed royalty. He already knew he married a queen, yet her command rang empress. The curly hair sat on the top of her head in a high puff that reminded him of a crown. Large eyes watched him and hundreds watched her.

He wasn't expecting such a grand entrance and believed it wasn't her plan to give one, yet here they were. Tyler felt his heart beat wildly in his chest as she appeared to float toward him. It wouldn't have surprised him if music started to play and he was close to sure that it was because heavenly harps seemed to breach his ears as she got closer.

Finally, she arrived and her closeness rattled him. Placing her arms around his back, she brought her lips to his ear and whispered. A smile stretched the corners of his mouth and he sighed. Kissing him on the cheek, Melody walked toward her mother in law who anxiously awaited her daughter's company.

"Turn your bibles to Isaiah 54. I am reading the English Standard Version verses sixteen through seventeen. Before I begin, I would like to say, my wife for life, Melody Deen, accepts my apology and we will be in Pennsylvania in thirty days. Let the church say amen." Tyler smiled sending Green Pastures into celebration.

www.ingramcontent.com/pod-product-compliance
Lightning Source LLC
Chambersburg PA
CBHW070021260626
47159CB00005B/1900